D1029506

Black Madonna

Also by Jacynth Hope-Simpson

Who Knows? Twelve Unsolved Mysteries

Black Madonna

Jacynth Hope-Simpson

THOMAS NELSON INC., PUBLISHERS
Nashville • New York

No character in this book is intended to represent any actual person; all the incidents of the story are entirely fictional in nature.

All rights reserved under International and Pan-American Conventions. Published by Thomas Nelson Inc., Publishers, Nashville, Tennessee. Manufactured in the United States of America.

First U.S. edition

Library of Congress Cataloging in Publication Data

Hope-Simpson, Jacynth.
  Black madonna.

  SUMMARY: Two teenage boys vacationing in Yugoslavia discover a priceless icon which becomes the target of art smugglers.
  [1. Icons—Fiction. 2. Yugoslavia—Fiction. 3. Adventure stories] I. Title.
PZ7.H7727Bl3   [Fic]   76-27315
ISBN 0-8407-6516-9

Black Madonna

1

Roger had stayed for judo, and Stephen had been proposing the motion in a debate. In those simple facts lay all the difference between them.

They hesitated because the door was not quite wide enough for them to go out side by side. If it had been a few inches wider, they might very well have gone on their separate ways without speaking, without even acknowledging one another.

It is possible, provided your school is enormous enough to get to within the last weeks of your school life without having any real contact with other boys in the same year as yourself. Stephen and Roger had always been in different classes, and their interests did not coincide. Nonetheless, each knew very well who the other was.

Everybody knew Roger. At six foot, with an enormous mop of fair hair and giving an impression of abundant physical energy, it was hard to miss him. He could be seen on Friday evenings, clad in extraordinary-looking clothes, as he waited for the school minibus which would take a small group of enthusiasts to crawl down caves in Derbyshire, or scramble up mountains in Wales. To many of the younger boys, he was a figure second in importance only to the star in the town's football team. Stephen was much less remarkable looking—dark-haired, with an air of untidiness that was caused, on examination, by the fact that his face seemed to be all nose and eyes, and the features had not quite settled down in relation to one another. In middle age, he might start to look distinguished. He hoped to go to the university in the autumn to study Russian, a thing that no other boy from the school had done before. Given his record at school, nobody really doubted that he would get there.

There could be no two boys in the school with less to say to each other.

Nonetheless, they were both basically kind-hearted boys, with good manners of a casual sort, so instead of pushing out through the door together, Roger said, "Go on," and Stephen said, "Thanks." Conversation might have stopped short at this uninspiring point if it had not occurred to both independently that it was rather defeatist for two of the leading personalities in the school not to make a little more effort to get to know one another.

So Roger went so far as to say, "It's raining."

"Yes, it is, isn't it?" said Stephen.

Once again, the dialogue halted, then Stephen said, more spontaneously, "Can I give you a lift? I think you live in my direction."

"I wouldn't mind," said Roger.

They went together toward the twelfth-grade parking lot. Here, the older pupils kept a strange assortment of vehicles that ranged from a beach buggy with homemade body work to an almost new Jaguar that had made the entire teaching staff declare that they were in the wrong profession. Stephen's contribution was a small compact car, eight years old. He sat in the driver's seat, started and stalled, started and stalled again, then reversed rather too quickly in the direction of the bicycle shed.

"I only passed the test last week." he said, excusing himself, as they crawled slowly through the school gates without further mishap.

"Did you pass the first time?"

"Yes. My instructor couldn't believe it. Didn't you get into the area finals of the Driver of the Year competition?"

"Yes. I just missed getting through to the national finals, though. What I need now is a car. I did two weeks on a building site at Easter, lugging cinder blocks around. Tiring and boring, but the money was good. They can give me another two or three weeks' work this summer, so I may make enough to buy one."

"Are you going away at all?" Stephen asked, as he stopped with a jerk by a red traffic light.

"That's the trouble. I want to go to this rock-climbing course on Skye, but it's during the first part of the holidays, when I'll be on this job."

They drove on through streets that were typical of a Yorkshire manufacturing town with terraced houses, long brick walls of factories, chimneys rising up from the misty valley below. Then they were caught in a traffic jam outside one of the town's largest plants, an engineering firm with an international reputation.

"My dad works for them," said Stephen. "Machinery for hydroelectric plants is his line, and he travels around to where it's being installed. He's just gone out to Yugoslavia to a dam site."

"Lots of limestone in Yugoslavia," Roger remarked.

When Stephen looked a little surprised at this observation, he added, "That means underground rivers. You get a river as wide as the Thames coming straight out of the rock. Should be a good place for caving. They have these gorges, too, for canoeing. I wouldn't mind going there."

"I could go if I wanted to. Go out and stay with Dad. Mom keeps on trying to persuade me to go. My married sister is going to have her first baby in August, and she wants me and Dad out of the way. My brother-in-law says he thinks she wants him out of the way as well."

"Why don't you go then?"

"Well, oh, you see, it's like this," said Stephen. "I passed the test the evening before Dad went. He said he'd pay for the gas if I drove out there. But I don't think he knows what my driving is really like. It's two thousand miles odd to where he is, right down on the Greek border. I don't guarantee I would get any farther than Calais."

"You couldn't do it alone," said Roger. "On a trip like that, you've got to have two drivers for safety. Don't any of your friends want to go?"

"None of the ones who might like to go has a license."

"What you need now is lots of practice," said Roger. "If you could go with someone a bit more experienced than yourself, you would soon get enough confidence. This is where I get out. Thanks for the lift."

"Be seeing you," said Stephen.

"Yes," said Roger. "You will."

In fact, they met in the corridor two days later.

"How old are you?" said Roger, without any preamble.

"Eighteen in August. Why?"

"My dad's got a friend who works in the Motor Vehicle

Bureau. He says you can't use your license abroad until you're eighteen. What date is your birthday?"

"The fifteenth."

"I come off the building site two days before that. I'm all right. My birthday was last week."

The next day, they met again. Stephen said, "I've been working it out. You'd have to allow a week each way for the journey, including the time it would take to get to the channel port. But will there be time enough if we wait till halfway through the holidays?"

"Not if we were going back to high school, or starting a job. But you're going to the university, aren't you, and they start term much later. And I'm going to college, if I pass my exams."

When Stephen did not entirely succeed in hiding his look of surprise, Roger grinned and added, "I want to be a phys ed instructor, or join an explorers' team. So I've got to get a degree in physical education first."

On Monday, in the cloakroom, Stephen said, "We'd have to camp, of course. We could never afford it otherwise. You know all about that, don't you?"

"Yes, and I've got most of the stuff that we'd need. It means getting a list of continental camp sites. And there's all sorts of documents for the car, and I don't know what else."

"Look, I'll do the car side of things if you like. Plan the routes, get the insurance, book us across the Channel. You deal with the camping. Sleeping things, cooking stove, what food we take and what it is best to buy over there."

It did not strike either of them as odd that, at no point, had they actually agreed to go together.

11

Everyone else in the twelfth grade thought it was very odd indeed. Stephen's friends all said that Stephen would be bored to death by Roger, who seldom talked about anything except climbing, canoeing, and girls. He would, they assured Stephen, be completely uninterested in the sort of thing that any intelligent person, meaning themselves, would look for in Yugoslavia, such as the after-effects of earthquakes, communism in action, and ancient Roman remains.

Roger's crowd said, a little obscurely, that Stephen would lose his head in emergencies.

"What sort of emergencies?" Roger wanted to know. "Like the car being chased by a pack of ravenous wolves?"

"There *are* wolves in Yugoslavia," said a boy who was majoring in geography. "And bears, too, up in the mountains."

"And secret police."

"They put you in prison first, and then ask questions afterwards."

"Be careful where you take photographs. Avoid airfields and military installations."

"And the Albanian border. Albania is more or less run by the Chinese, and the two countries are on bad terms."

Faced with the prospect of secret police, wolves, and earthquakes, none of which Roger minded nearly so much as the thought of Roman remains, both boys set out to find out more about the country. What they sought to find was typical of themselves.

Roger read about rivers flowing through deep gorges, and how you could travel down them on rafts made of logs; of wide streams that poured out of limestone cliffs, and then, a few miles later, plunged into deep underground courses again, to be lost for ever. He looked longingly at his wet suit and caving helmet, and wondered how he could justify to Stephen the space that these, and a long coil of rope, would take up in the compact car. In the end, he left them behind, for it would not be safe to go cave exploring alone, and he could not imagine Stephen as a companion. Then he read of Lake Ohrid, where there are fish that are survivors of prehistoric times, and, though he was not interested in fish, this reminded him to pack his face mask and snorkel.

Meanwhile, Stephen tried to disentangle the past of a country that had, until this century, been a collection of different states, frequently attacked and often captured by foreign powers. The areas they would drive through had a variety both of languages and of religions. Stephen gave the villainous scowl he always produced when he was concentrating; it had been said that Stephen in an examination looked like someone escaped from a top-security prison. He read that the coast, the part most often visited by British tourists, had strong links with western Europe, but that the part of the country where they would be staying belonged much more to the East. It would seem to have some things in common with Russia, the foreign country in which he was most interested.

Like Russia, southern Yugoslavia had belonged to the Eastern Orthodox Church for nearly a thousand years. It had drawn its traditions from the city once called Byzantium, then Constantinople, and now known as Istanbul. In both countries, especially in the churches, some traces of Byzantium still remained.

Stephen took a book on Byzantine art out of the public library. He learned that the Orthodox Church does not allow statues, so all art was flat—either wall paintings or mosaics, or smaller pictures called icons, which were set on a screen that hid the altar completely. He read, with due skepticism, that the icons were not merely pictures of holy things, but were thought of as being holy in themselves, and that some were credited with working miracles.

They were odd pictures, thought Stephen, who knew little about art. If you expected paintings to look like real life, they were rather bad, being stiff and flat. If you accepted the modern idea of pictures as pattern and decoration, there might be something in them. He reserved his judgment until he could see them in the flesh, and turned to working out the price of gasoline in West Germany.

At last, they were ready to have a trial run of packing the car, with friends of both parties attending to make unhelpful suggestions. They were given stickers to put on the car, so many that they would have hidden all view through the back window. Stephen put them instead on the inside walls.

"How about the outside?" somebody asked. "You could at least have a sign of what you are. "Thornfields School Graduates' Expedition to . . . how do you spell Yugoslavia, anyhow? Is it a *Y* or a *J?*"

"Either," said Stephen. "In the Yugoslav languages, *j* is pronounced like a *y*.

"What do you mean, languages? I thought they spoke Serbo-Cruet."

"*Croat*, you idiot," said the geography expert.

"They have four official languages, and at least three unofficial ones," said Stephen, who was glad to show off his newly acquired knowledge. "Serbian and Croatian sound very similar, but Croatian is written in our sort of alphabet and Serbian in an alphabet called Cyrillic."

14

"Extraordinary sort of country!" said someone.

"Do you think that those bears will eat them?"

"No, but I bet that they'll be arrested."

"Or get into a fight over a girl. This guidebooks says that the women are beautiful, and the men are full of warlike fervor. You'd better watch out, Roger."

"It is probably exactly like Yorkshire," said Roger in an effort to quiet them down.

Whatever else might be said of Yugoslavia, it was not in the least like Yorkshire.

2

While Roger and Stephen made their fumbling and thoroughly amateur plans, a much more professional trip to Yugoslavia was also being discussed. First, neither of the two men concerned had any intention of traveling on his own passport.

The older of the two was a man called Klaus, a Swiss citizen of respectable appearance and good reputation. He lived in a neat, modern villa overlooking the Lake of Zürich, and his whole way of life was a balance between being obviously very well off and not spending money wastefully, both qualities which the Swiss admire. He looked young enough to seem enterprising, and just middle-aged enough for older people to trust him. His clothes were expensive, their style traditional but not too conservative; his car, a large silver-gray Mercedes, was fast but in no way flashy. He gave liberally to that charity so beloved of the Swiss, the Red Cross.

Zürich is one of the chief financial centers in the world, and reputedly one of the world's richest cities. Klaus was known and respected both by his fellow citizens and by many of the foreign businessmen who visited the city. His profession was that of an art dealer who specialized in Italian paintings. His customers always said how well he knew their individual tastes, so he would explain to them that he kept detailed lists. For example, he told them, the customers who collected eighteenth-century paintings were on List 6, and those who specialized in pictures from Naples were on List 11. He never made any mention of List 17.

List 17, which was filed in his villa and not in the office, was headed "Ready cash always available." Precisely three other people knew that it also meant that the customers on it would happily buy a painting that had been stolen, and would not ask any questions about it.

It was Klaus's air of respectability, and the fact that he had such a reputation for being efficient, that gave a perfect cover to the dishonest side of his business. Unfortunately for himself, he was proving a little too successful. As the value of money itself fell, more and more rich businessmen were buying works of art as an investment. He was faced with more demands from customers than he could possibly satisfy, especially since he took very good care, for the sake of safety, to limit the number of stolen pictures he handled. He was faced with the long-term risk that the supply of Italian pictures might start to dry up. He therefore decided to branch out into another field.

Klaus wanted a form of art that was sought after, that was increasing in value, but which few other dealers could offer. He also wanted pictures of which he could obtain what he termed "an additional supply" for his List 17 customers. In Klaus's experience, much the easiest place

17

to steal paintings from was a church, which tended to be less well guarded than either a public or private collection. Frequently, since churches are often badly lighted, the paintings were also much less well known. After a great deal of thought he decided to open a new, small gallery for the sale of icons.

The gallery, he hoped, would be called Iconostasis, which is the name for the altar screen in an Orthodox church on which icons are displayed. There were two factors in his choice. One was that icons were becoming very popular with the West German collectors who were some of his wealthiest customers. The other was that during his researches he had read an article on icons in Yugoslavia by a Dr. Petar Metkovic, Assistant Keeper of Byzantine art in the National Museum in Belgrade. One sentence had struck clearly in his mind.

"In addition to well-known collections of icons, such as those at Decani Monastery, Saint Kliment, Ohrid, and the Monastery of the Mother of God, there are almost certainly others, not yet catalogued by scholars, in remote churches and monasteries in southern Yugoslavia, many of which are still only accessible by foot or on horseback."

Klaus could not ride a horse, but as a health-conscious Swiss he reckoned that he was quite a good walker. His intention was to get hold of some of those icons before Dr. Metkovic or anyone like him had a chance to examine them.

After much thought he decided to go and investigate for himself. In Italy, he employed a gang of established art thieves and had never had any personal contact with what he called "the operational side" of the matter. Klaus was, by habit, so cautious that he never described his activities in straight language, even in his own thoughts. He told himself that he would be interested to be "out in the field" for a change. What this really meant was that he was tired of sitting in an office, making plans, and that he wanted the stimulus of actually doing something. He did not recognize that this might be a dangerous state of mind.

He chose as his companion a young man called Heinrich, who was the firm's restorer and one of the three in Klaus's full confidence. Henrich was a very clever restorer, which meant he could paint in many different styles. Klaus was fully aware that he earned another income by the sale of skillful forgeries, and it was for this reason that he wanted his company in Yugoslavia.

The Italian thieves worked by cutting canvases out of frames and then putting them in suitcases with false bottoms, hollow spaces in high-backed car seats, and many other such hiding places. Icons could not be hidden in such a way for the very simple reason that they were painted on thick panels of wood. They were heavy and bulky, and could not be rolled up. Klaus thought that he saw a way out of the difficulties.

He would set himself up as a dealer in modern copies of icons, as sold in high-class gift shops. They would be quite good copies, with realistic fake wormholes, but would make no pretense of fooling an expert. He, or somebody acting for him, would enter Yugoslavia with an import license for his copies. During the trip, these copies would be left in churches, as a substitute for the same number of original icons. He would then leave, by a different border point, using the license to take the stolen works out. If the customs officials asked why he had not sold anything, he would explain that they were only trade samples.

His plan was, of course, that Heinrich should paint the copies. This first trip was to be in the nature of a reconnaissance. They would see what was available, and they would take a great many photographs from which Henrich could work. The whole of Klaus's success had been built up by careful planning and by not rushing anything.

It was August before they were ready to go. They flew from Zürich to Milan on their own passports, and the airport police at Zürich, who knew Klaus as a regular traveler, greeted him and wished him a successful journey. In Milan, at a house recommended to them as having a very quiet and discreet owner, they set about to change their identities.

Klaus did not need to do very much. The barber, whom he had asked to come, cut his hair so that it looked much thinner, and this made him seem older. He removed his contact lenses and put on a pair of glasses with thin metal frames, so again he looked older and much less prosperous. He exchanged his extremely expensive clothes for a medium-quality, ready-made suit, which almost, but not quite, fitted. His handmade shoes were exchanged for a pair from a chain store, and his Rolex chronometer for a mass-production watch. Though he still looked respectable, and by no means poor, he was no longer the sort of man to whom headwaiters hurry to give the best table. His mother would have known him at a glance, but casual acquaintances might have been puzzled.

Heinrich needed a great deal more work to be done on him. Since he regarded himself as an artist, and not a businessman, he belonged to the beard, beads, and frayed-jeans school of dress. The loss of his beard and most of his hair produced many protests from him. He was put, still objecting loudly, into a drip-dry shirt, drip-dry tie, and drip-dry suit. They were then both photographed in their new identities. Next day they were provided with forged Swiss passports, which had been prepared but were awaiting the photographs. Klaus's said that he was a gift-shop owner, and Heinrich's that he was a management trainee.

Finally, they took possession of a hired white Fiat of medium size, which in southern Europe was just about as unremarkable as a car could be. They had documents for driving the car into Yugoslavia via Trieste, and tickets for bringing it back on the ferry from Dubrovnik in Yugoslavia to Ancona in Italy. They slung a battery of cameras over their shoulders, including a Polaroid for instant pictures, and one, which they had brought from Switzerland, with a top-quality lens, which the salesman had assured them would photograph "a black man in a coal cellar by night." This was for taking the photographs from which Heinrich would later work.

Once in Yugoslavia, they drove down the main route to Belgrade, and then began to wander in search of little churches and of monasteries where only a handful of monks remained. They drove over tracks that made them fear for the springs of the car, and occasionally Klaus walked in front in order to make out on which bit of the mountainside the track actually was. He decided that if he came again he would have to have a car with a four-wheel drive. All the time they took photographs, and the list of icons that seemed worth copying and then

21

stealing was neatly disguised in a photographer's record book.

Their southernmost point was Ohrid, near the Greek frontier. The other visitors in their hotel soon learned to avoid them. It was almost as boring to have Heinrich show twenty Polaroid photographs of Lake Ohrid at sunset as it was to hear Klaus talking about the economics of selling cuckoo clocks. They passed as uncle and nephew, and Klaus was only too willing to tell anybody his doubts as to whether Heinrich would ever make a good businessman.

By this point, they were feeling reasonably happy about their plans. They had found many little-used churches, most of which were extremely dark, because Eastern churches, unlike those of western Europe, have very few windows, and those small and set high in the walls. The churches were lighted by candles, if lighted at all. Heinrich had been worried about doing paintings that would pass a close scrutiny, because Byzantine art is a specialized form of painting, and he had no close knowledge of it. He now became confident that he could paint copies that would be convincing in such a poor light.

Klaus began to find himself unusually relaxed. The hotels in which they stayed were, to his Swiss eyes, abominable, and for several days he cursed both the food and the plumbing. He could not buy a newspaper written in any language he understood, and he missed the endless relays of teleprinted tape that keep the citizens of Zürich up to date with share prices. Then, suddenly, he found he was glad to miss them. This was the first time in many years that he had had a complete break from business. He began to think that when the forgeries were ready, he himself would like to come back to do the actual stealing. Perhaps, he thought, he was not really a planner, but a man of action instead. It did not occur to him that if he stepped right out of his usual role he might find himself in a situation he could not handle.

Heinrich, too, had his concentration threatened. In his case it was because he found himself so interested in the actual paintings that he sometimes forgot what they had come for.

They left Ohrid and drove north again, on their journey to Dubrovnik, from where they would get the ferry to Italy. At Heinrich's insistence, they planned to visit several monasteries that were still in use. He wanted to see the paintings there, even if there would never be any prospect of stealing them.

He planned to visit Cecani, and the Monastery of the Mother of God, which was near a small town called Starigrad. This dictated their route. They would drive to Starigrad, and then take the new road over the mountains, avoiding the old road through the Kurnovo gorge, which their guidebook described as "perhaps the worst road in Europe."

Everything was going according to their carefully laid plans. They set out full of confidence.

3

Roger and Stephen drove eastward and southward, then southward and eastward again. Their way took them past smoking industrial cities, and through monotonous forest where for hour after hour the only view was of fir trees on either side of the highway. At last they crossed over the Alps, and still they drove on. They began to have the strange illusion that they had been driving for ever, and were condemned never to stop. When Stephen shut his eyes at night, all he could see was road stretching ahead.

They drove on through Belgrade, the Yugoslav capital. By now, the road was much worse. The E5, the European through-route which they were following, was no longer a highway, but an ordinary two-lane road. With the sun at its height blazing down on the little car, they found themselves stuck behind a house trailer on a long hill. They shut the window because of clouds of exhaust.

"How much farther?" asked Roger, in a tone that implied that all adventure had gone from their journey, and only endurance remained.

"Well over another hundred miles on this road. Nearly down to the Greek frontier. Then we turn right onto a minor road. Let's hope there won't be so much traffic."

More trailers thundered downhill toward them, making it hopeless to try to pass. Stephen, who was driving, felt the engine shudder.

"Downshift. You should have before now." said Roger. In spite of good resolutions he had often found it hard not to criticize Stephen's driving.

They ground on over the brow of the hill. A few hundred yards later, Stephen suddenly turned off on a minor road to the right. There was no other traffic, and within a few hundred yards they seemed to be many miles away from the busy main road.

All around them stretched fields where groups of people were working, raking in the last of the grain harvest and piling it onto carts pulled by ponderous white oxen. They all wore national dress, and the women seemed to move slowly and very deliberately beneath the weight of their clothes. They drove past a group of gypsies by the side of the road. They wore clothes that clung to their lithe bodies, and which were made of faded materials that had once been vivid. Their movements were much quicker and more fluid than those of the peasants working around them.

A little farther along, some water buffalo were wallowing in a deep muddy pond. Only their nostrils, their bulging eyes, and their horns showed above the surface.

"I grant you that this is a much more pleasant road, but will it get us to where we are going?" asked Roger when they came to a signpost.

"Yes, it goes to a town called Starigrad. There, we turn south. We will be doing two sides of a square. If we

25

had stayed on the main road, we would have done the other two sides."

"But the sign doesn't say 'Starigrad.' It doesn't say anything. The letters aren't proper letters."

"It's the alphabet they use in southern Yugoslavia. It is very much like the Russian alphabet, which is how I can read it."

For the first time, Roger looked at Stephen with real respect.

It was early evening as they drove toward Starigrad. About ten miles from the town, they began to meet many carts that were returning from the market. They were laden high with vegetables—shiny peppers and eggplants—with bundles of wool, carded but not yet spun, that looked like small, fluffy clouds; and with lambs, calves, pigs and hens, squealing and squawking away.

Whole families were piled on the carts, all wearing national costume. There were so many variations that it seemed as if each small village must have its own dress. Cart after cart came on, in dozens and then hundreds. Stephen felt as if he and Roger, in their car and their western clothes, were out of place.

Then they saw the outline of Starigrad against the pink and gold of the evening sky. Tall, thin lines of poplars punctuated the roofs, and echoing the shape of the poplars were the narrow pointed spires of dozens of minarets.

"Look here, what is this place?" asked Roger. "Are we in Europe, or aren't we?"

"Yes and no. What happened is that six hundred years ago, the Turks conquered all the country around here. It was Christian before that, but they made it largely Muslim. That's why there are all those mosques in the town ahead."

"What happened after they conquered it?"

"Nothing happened for over five hundred years. The rest of Europe went ahead, but the people here remained stuck in the Middle Ages."

"They're still stuck there," said Roger, as they entered the town. They drove between houses hidden by high, blank walls as if they were fortified. The only way in was by huge wooden doors, blanched by years of weathering, that had heavy, ornate knockers. Some women in flowing skirts, with witchlike strands of black hair showing beneath their head scarves, squatted in the gutter talking to one another with great animation. The road was dusty and covered with animal dung.

"What a way to live!" exclaimed Roger.

"Maybe it's better to sit in the gutter and talk to your friends than to live on the twentieth floor of a high-rise apartment building and not know your neighbors." said Stephen slowly.

It was getting harder and and harder to drive, for as well as the carts on the move, there were more carts by the roadside. Literally thousands of people must have come in to market. The street became narrower, and the upper floors of the houses overhung it. They glimpsed groups of women peering at them through the latticed windows of first-floor rooms.

They drove past a little graveyard which, with a strangely inconsequential air, was placed by the edge of the road in between the houses. The tombs were short, stubby pillars with carved turbans on top, and most of them were leaning over. On the other side of the road was a large stone building with little domes all over the roof, which Stephen surmised was a Turkish bathhouse.

The press of traffic was soon so dense that they were unable to move. All around them was this odd mixture of liveliness on one hand, decay and neglect on the other.

27

They crawled on for another few yards, then were stuck behind a parked cart.

From somewhere near they heard the sound of music, an almost hypnotic rhythm struck without pause on several tambourines at once. Somebody opened a door in the wall beside them, and they caught a glimpse of what seemed to be a wedding. A girl in white was sitting upon a dais, and in front of her several other girls, also in white heavily trimmed with gold, gyrated in a slow, deliberate dance. A crowd of women and girls were inside, drinking and talking, and then the door was shut and the scene went blank.

"There's a camp just south of Starigrad—if we ever get there," said Roger. He seemed determined to keep a hold on the ordinary and familiar, and not give way to the illusion that they had stepped backward in time.

The door was opened once again, and still the music and the dancing went on. Two girls came out and clambered onto the parked cart. They were both about fifteen years old and wore blouses with very full sleeves and strange trousers, made of yard after yard of material, falling in folds from the waist, and gathered together a little above the ankles. Their heads were covered with gauzy scarves, which, at the sight of the boys, they pulled over their faces. Two large black eyes, one eye per girl, peered out.

"Nobody ever told me," said Roger rather obscurely. What he actually meant was that, after years of seeing girls in miniskirts, girls in bikinis, and girls in tennis outfits, nothing had prepared him for the devastating effect of girls almost totally muffled up.

The cart drove off. Both boys were vaguely aware that it was being controlled by a skinny boy who had also come from the wedding party, but neither of them had any interest in him. They goggled at the two girls, who gazed demurely, and rather smugly, back, and when Stephen's steering wobbled, Roger did not even notice.

They approached the outskirts of the town, and from somewhere over their heads came the high-pitched, wailing cry of a muezzin, a Muslim crier, calling the faithful to prayer.

Still the procession of carts rumbled on, ahead of them and behind them. At last, they came to a crossroads on the outskirts of the town. The road straight ahead seemed to be no more than a dirt track, and bore a faded sign saying "Bogorodica Monastery." The road to the right, up which many carts were turning, led, Stephen noticed, in the direction of Titograd and ultimately to the coast. The left-hand turn to Ohrid was the one he wanted himself.

The cart with the two girls made its slow way over the crossroads toward the dirt track, stopping to let someone on foot go past. With elaborate winking and hand signals, Stephen prepared to turn left. Halfway through the maneuver he realized that he was setting out to drive on the left-hand side of the road in the British manner, and he ought to be on the right. He overcorrected and swerved. He was conscious of the two girls staring at him and felt foolish, so in a fit of rather defiant bravado he gave them a couple of loud farewell toots on his horn. At this the horse shied, and the cart lunged backward.

The car was by now at right angles to the cart. Stephen was in a panic. He tried to brake and swerve simultaneously, but merely cut his engine. There was a loud grating noise as a piece of metal protruding from the back of the cart struck the rear corner of the car. Stephen, trembling a little, climbed out, leaving Roger to put on the handbrake.

The actual damage was not very great, but the rear

29

and brake lights had shattered. While Stephen was looking at this, the boy who had been driving clambered along to the end of the cart, and stood with his hands on his hips gazing down at Stephen contemptuously. Stephen started to say, "I'm sorry," but his voice was drowned out by the boy's.

"You stupid, incompetent fool," he said in English. "Sounding your horn like that and scaring the horse. That's what I'd call typically English behavior. Coming to other people's countries and behaving as if you owned them."

Stephen was conscious of several emotions at once. One was indignation. If there was to be an argument, the boy had an unfair advantage by being higher up. Another was astonishment that this boy should speak English, and that in an accent almost arrogantly correct and pure. Roger scrambled out of the car and come to his rescue.

"You can't blame Stephen entirely," he said in tones as if he himself had never been tempted to criticize Stephen's driving. "If you hadn't stopped, it would never have happened. And you oughtn't to drive a horse if you can't control it."

"At least I had my mind on the horse. What were you doing? Gazing at the twins, I suppose, as if they were a bar of chocolate, and you were somebody in a television commercial." He gave a withering look at the boys and the twins alike. The twins, clearly perfectly happy to be the center of any form of attention, whispered to one another behind their veils.

"That doesn't get over the fact that it was your cart that hit my car," put in Stephen.

The boy promptly switched his attack.

"Can't you see that you're blocking the traffic, and getting in everyone's way? Follow me off the road."

Without stopping for an answer, or without even bothering to sit down again, he drove the cart a little way up the dirt track. When he stood holding the reins he looked like a Greek charioteer. His hair, which was cut short, much shorter than Stephen's or Roger's, gleamed reddish, reminding Stephen of a bronze statue in the last of the evening sun. He was dressed in national costume from the waist up. A coarse linen shirt under a jerkin came to the top of his thighs, and beneath that, rather more prosaically, he wore a pair of shabby blue jeans. With his self-assured air and his command of English it was hard to be sure what he was—a local peasant who had adopted the international fashion for jeans, or somebody from the outer world who shared the widespread feeling among teenagers for "ethnic" clothes.

"What a conceited boy," Stephen muttered to Roger. "But you have to admit he speaks English uncommonly well."

"He's a peculiar sort of boy altogether," said Roger, rather more loudly. The boy heard him and stood for a moment, frowning and looking thoughtful. Then he jumped lightly down from the cart and went to inspect the damage.

"It's hurt your car more than it's hurt Mr. Mustapha's cart. It could be the local cartmaker does a better job than the British production line."

"What have you got against England?" asked Stephen crossly.

The boy ignored him.

"You know that you mustn't drive tonight without a light on your car in case the cops get you. And it will be dark soon, too. Where were you planning to go?"

"We're looking for a camp site," Roger said rather stiffly.

"You'd better come home with me and camp in our orchard. Then tomorrow we'll see about getting your

31

lights mended."

Having asserted a mastery over the two English boys, who, so far as they could tell, were several years older than he was, the boy appeared to relax. The two girls who had been listening without, it would seem, being able to understand a word, gazed at him admiringly whenever he spoke English. One of them giggled a little, and murmured a name that sounded like Joey.

"Are you called Joey?" asked Roger.

The boy drew together his narrow eyebrows, which lay over very deep-set eyes. In a voice that was rather low for a boy, but was by no means that of a man, he said, "Approximately."

Stephen privately thought that this was an odd name for a Yugoslav boy, but then, as Roger had pointed out, this boy was odd altogether. In any case, he remembered, the President of Yugoslavia, Marshal Tito, was called Joseph. Aloud, he said, "I'm Stephen, and this is Roger."

"I'll come in the car and direct you, and the twins can drive home. It's their grandfather's cart," said Joey. He picked up the reins and tossed it to one of the twins. As she caught it, her veil slipped, and the boys caught a glimpse of a pretty, vivid face with very white teeth.

"Drive straight up the road," said Joey.

The road, no more than a cart track, led up a wide valley. Some way ahead, the valley narrowed and then seemed to come to an end with a wall of high mountains. As the evening light faded, the mountains lost all solidity and became only a jagged pattern against the sky. The fields around them were dotted with haystacks, shaped like witches' hats. They could make out the shape of a minaret, like a tall, narrow candle among the trees, and, a little distance away from it, the dome of a tiny church. There was no one in sight except for a small boy driving a flock of goats.

For several minutes none of them spoke, and then Roger, with one subject on his mind, said, "The twins? I mean—how do we take it? We're not used to veils and all that."

"Keep off the twins," said Joey.

"I don't think that that was the twins' idea," Stephen pointed out mildly.

"That pair need spanking!" said Joey, in a voice that made it hard to remember that he must, if anything, be younger than were the twins. Stephen wondered in just what circumstances he was allowed to go out with them. "But, seriously, look out. The twins' grandfather, Mr. Mustapha, is a strict, old-fashioned Muslim, and treats his family accordingly. During the war, there was a German soldier who fancied the twins' mother. Mr. Mustapha still keeps his cap badge and buttons up on a shelf in the kitchen."

"What became of him?"

"You're not saying. . . ?"

Joey shrugged.

"Look, while you're here you'd better forget any make-love-not-war ideas. We don't have that sort of history. Mr. Mustapha and my grandfather have both fought in three wars. When they were only twelve, they fought in the Balkan War, which turned the Turks out of our country. Mr. Mustapha, being a Muslim, fought for the Turks that time. Then the First World War was triggered off in Sarajevo, not much over a hundred miles from here. So they joined up to fight the Germans, being veterans of fourteen. Then, during the Second World War, the Germans invaded again. This time they became guerrillas, and joined Tito's partisans.

"Nowadays, more or less all they do, and it nearly

33

drives my mother and the twins' mother crazy, is to sit around drinking Granddad's homemade *raki* and boasting to one another about how many Germans they killed. But supposing an enemy tank ever came driving up this cart track. Those two would rise from their deathbeds, if necessary, to throw homemade gasoline bombs at it. Stephen, take the next turn to the left."

With considerable doubt as to what they had let themselves in for, Stephen drove up a narrow track between fields of corn. They came to a house, a solid, square building set in a plum orchard, with a row of outbuildings at right angles to it. In the evening air a number of different and distinctive smells came from the outbuildings. Stephen identified the smell of animals, perhaps oxen, in a stable; the pungent, faintly sweet scent of long lines of tobacco hung up to dry; and then an unfamiliar, powerful, heady smell.

"Granddad's distillery," said Joey. "The end product is a cross between dynamite and sulfuric acid, but he seems to thrive on it."

"Ought Mr. Mustapha to drink it? I thought Muslims didn't," said Stephen.

"They don't drink wine. The Koran never foresaw Granddad's *raki.*"

He led them to where two old men were sitting beneath a plum tree. They had been playing some game with pebbles as counters, but now that the light had faded they were mainly concerned with the contents of a very large bottle. They looked at the boys with interest, and then, dismissing Stephen as of little account, they concentrated on Roger. In the end, they dismissed him too, as if somehow aware that he had never killed anybody.

The one introduced as Granddad was, like Joey, dressed in national costume down to the waist and Western trousers below. Mr. Mustapha reversed the procedure. He wore a shabby jacket and shirt that might once have belonged to a waiter, but beneath that he had loose trousers of unbleached wool that were embroidered with braid and set very low on the hips. On his head he wore a skullcap of white felt, which gave his head a gleaming, bald look, and imparted to his whole face a look of malevolence. There was still something strangely formidable about the two ancient warriors, rather like Odysseus in old age, thought Stephen.

Joey spoke to them in Serbian, and they answered in the same language. Stephen noticed that they spoke his name with the *j*-sound soft and slurred as in French. Then, with another of his imperious nods, Joey led the two English boys into the house.

"Wait here while I fetch my mother."

As he went out, he switched on an electric light. They examined their surroundings by what seemed this almost incongruous link with the normal, modern world.

The room was large, with a cobbled stone floor and a fine, carved ceiling. There was a long wooden table, set with copper bowls and very thick pottery, with rush-seated chairs around it. Everything looked old, used, and very well kept. The boys were vaguely aware that, in England, people paid a great deal to achieve an effect like this.

What completely removed it from the *Ideal Homes* atmosphere were the pictures. The largest was of Marshal Tito, the President of Yugoslavia, in uniform and medals. Then came a faded sepia photograph of a very young boy, presumably Granddad, in the uniform of the First World War. Next to it was a large niche in the wall, which seemed made to contain the most important picture of all, but which at the moment was empty.

35

On the other side of Tito's portrait was a whole row of photographs—four boys, all in shabby clothes, carrying guns and wearing a star on the breast of their ragged jackets.

"This one, the youngest, with hand grenades slung around his waist, reminds me of Joey," said Roger. He pointed toward the photograph of a boy who had the dedicated look of the young fanatic.

"Who on earth is this, though?" said Stephen.

The last photograph was that of a man in the full dress uniform of a Scottish Highland regiment. They stared at it in astonishment until a voice from behind them said, "Sergeant Duncan MacLeod, Argyll and Sutherland Highlanders. He was my husband."

They turned around and saw a rather tall woman with dark hair that was going gray, who had the same facial structure and the same deep-set eyes as Joey. She was dressed quite unremarkably in a blouse and skirt that might have come from any chain store in Europe, but she gave a great impression of natural dignity.

She said in English that was correct but heavily accented, "I am Marya MacLeod, Joey's mother."

"That explains it!" exclaimed Stephen. "Why Joey speaks English so well and yet hates the English."

"Oh, Joey's a Scottish Nationalist," said Mrs. MacLeod. She, too, spoke the name with the first letter slurred, but Stephen did not have time to register the pronunciation exactly before Roger spoke.

"I know I may be slow on the uptake, but please, just what is this setup?"

Mrs. MacLeod gave the half-smile of a woman who has not found a great deal in life to make her smile.

"It started during the last war. Your leader, Winston

Churchill, heard stories that there was a guerrilla leader in Yugoslavia whose forces were killing a lot of Germans. Nobody knew who he was. So Churchill sent in a British military mission to find out. They parachuted into the mountains. Their leader was Fitzroy Maclean, and my husband was with him as a radio operator.

"What they found was Marshal Tito. In those days, his clothes were dirty, and he lived in a cave. They found the partisans, who were middle-aged men like my father, and young boys like my brothers, even women and priests, as well as men of fighting age. They had no uniforms, and no elaborate weapons. But so many German divisions were tied up here fighting them that it helped change the course of the war.

"After the war, I got married, and we went back to Scotland to live. Then three years ago, my husband died. My two elder children decided to stay on in Scotland. I wanted to come back here myself, because my mother had died a few months before. Two of my brothers were killed with the partisans, and the third lost a leg, so there was nobody else to help Granddad with the farm."

"And Joey came with you," said Stephen. "In spite of being a Scottish Nationalist."

This time, Mrs. MacLeod smiled fully.

"You could hear the sound of protest from Glasgow to John O'Groats. But I said that I wanted one of my children to grow up in my own country, and go to school, and maybe to university, here. The funny thing is that Joey has now become a violent Yugoslav patriot."

Mrs. MacLeod turned away, and added as to herself, "I am not sure it is good for anyone to feel things as intensely as Joey."

4

They slept that night in the orchard, among all the sharp, unfamiliar smells. They had had supper in the farmhouse, for Mrs. MacLeod had offered to give them their main meals. Granddad, who spoke no word of English, had managed to dominate the whole conversation, and Joey or his mother had translated for him.

On hearing Stephen's name he had told long stories about a king called Stephen, who had been a very great man in those parts. Roger had assumed that he must have been the last king before Tito took over, but Stephen, with an odd crawling of the skin, realized that this man, of whom Granddad spoke as a familiar, had lived six hundred years ago.

Then Granddad had switched to stories about a bear that had been stealing his grapes, and how he and Mr. Mustapha planned to shoot it. The two English boys were not certain whether to believe him or not.

Stephen awoke late next morning, and found that Roger was gone.

He started to make his breakfast, and Joey appeared.

"We took your car into Starigrad, and we brought it back. They haven't got any spare parts there, and it means sending off to Skopje, or even Belgrade. So we've sent a telegram to your father to say that you will be delayed for a day or two. Luckily Roger had his address."

"Where is Roger?"

"He's gone off somewhere exploring. Hurry up with your breakfast, and then I'll show you around."

Joey's expression was faintly sardonic, and his manner seemed to imply that he was much older than Stephen, not only in terms of self-assurance, but in what he knew. Stephen, who suffered at home from having a very precocious younger brother, was prepared to be tolerant.

Their path took them past the little mosque that Stephen had noticed the night before. It was surrounded by trees and had a domed fountain in front of it, presumably for ritual washing before prayer. Just outside the mosque, under an overhanging roof, there was a stone platform on which several old men sat talking, their hands nursing the heads of their walking sticks.

"Are we allowed to go in?" asked Stephen.

"Yes, if you take your shoes off and leave them outside."

The floor of the mosque was covered with shabby carpets, a mixture of the cheap and what might well be valuable. There was nothing at all inside it except for an alcove where the altar might be in a church, a tall pulpit with very steep stairs, and a grandfather clock. The sun streamed in through bright-colored stained-glass windows, and lit up dancing specks of dust.

"How long did the Turks rule here?"

"Five hundred and twenty-three years," Joey said promptly. "From 1389 to 1912. When I first came here

39

everything seemed unendurably backward, even compared to the Highlands. I blamed the people for not having done anything to improve their conditions. And then I suddenly realized that, under the Turks, they didn't have any chance to. Time stood completely still."

"You mean to say you got stuck in the time of Chaucer?"

"That's right. We missed out on all the things that happened to other countries. The invention of printing and founding schools. Parliament and the voyages to America and the East. All the industrial things like machinery and railways and canals. None of these happened to us. We were so cut off from the rest of the world that we scarcely knew they existed. All we had to live on, for centuries, was the memory of our past."

"Like Granddad and King Stephen?"

"Exactly. You realize Granddad can't read? It was all handed down by ballads."

"You ought to go in for politics, the way you talk," said Stephen.

"I'd like to, if I have the chance. So long as I'm free to do what I want, and not have other people telling me what to do. That's what I care about."

Stephen felt something must lie behind this, but did not like to ask what.

They went a little farther on up the valley. On either side of the track were fields of giant sunflowers, which seemed to generate a light of their own, independent of the power of the sun. They came to a tiny church, a domed building of sunbaked brick, which had been half buried in the earth so that it did not offend the eyes of the Turkish invaders.

Joey glanced up at Stephen, almost embarrassed, as

40

if it mattered that Stephen should understand what they were about to see.

"This church is called Sveti Marko, which means 'Saint Mark.' It shows you what the country was like before the Turks conquered us. But don't expect something in perfect condition. It's been neglected for nearly six hundred years, because nobody had any money to spend on it. A friend of mine"—he hesitated oddly over the word—"called Petar Metkovic, who works for the National Museum in Belgrade, wants the state to take it over and restore it and turn it into a museum."

Stephen went in, and stepped into a different world.

It was the first time he had been in an Orthodox church. He had some idea of what to expect, but was not prepared for the impact that it would make.

Every single inch of the walls, from the floor to the dome, was covered with paintings. It was too dark to see what they were. Then, as his eyes adjusted, Stephen began to make out figures—priests in vestments, warriors, saints, Old Testament prophets. He saw evangelists, guarded by mythical beasts, apostles, the Virgin Mary, and, up in the dome, the stern face of Christ the judge. As the images surrounded him and soared over him, he came to have the feeling that he himself was nothing.

The sensation faded away, and he found himself in a shabby church, where all the lower frescoes were obscured by rising damp. In some places, the paint had been scorched by a forest of small, thin candles. The candles were stuck into sand, and around them were scattered some coins, so few and so tiny as to bring home the poverty of the place.

"Do you think it ought to be a museum?" Stephen asked Joey.

41

"No, I don't. But the trouble is that I don't believe in religion. Quite honestly, it all seems rather foolish to me. And so I can never explain to Petar just why it is I am so convinced he is wrong."

Before Stephen could decide what he felt himself, two other people came into the church. They were manifestly foreign tourists, in Dacron suits and festooned with cameras. They looked at the boys in some annoyance, which was quickly subdued, and began to take photographs. As they did so, they carefully measured exposures, angles, and distances, and made notes in a little book.

For some reason, Stephen preferred to identify himself with the church, rather than make it known to them that he was a foreigner too. He turned all his attention to the iconostasis, the screen of pictures that cut off the altar from the rest of the church.

He saw paintings of the Virgin and saints, done on gold backgrounds, that were not, Stephen suspected, paint, but a thin layer of the pure metal. They were stiff, rigid, and to his eyes unnatural, yet at the same time amazingly charged with emotion. The figures stared down at him with what looked like challenge in their dark eyes. They were muffled in heavy folds of drapery, with little flesh showing, but in the line of cheekbone and jaw, in the nervous intensity of the fingers, the skeleton was made plain.

The younger of the two newcomers caught his breath audibly. For a moment, he and Stephen were united, in knowing that they were in the presence of something remarkable. Then the young man made his face a deliberate blank.

Stephen peered behind the iconostasis to see what mysteries were hidden there. He knew that in the ritual of the Orthodox church this was the holiest place of all.

He saw an altar with a plastic lace tablecloth, a bucket, and an old step ladder. He noticed that the icons were only held into the screen by rusty, bent nails. This mixture of the sublime and the commonplace was disconcerting, yet oddly typical of human life as a whole.

Meanwhile, the two men were talking together, giving their conversation an almost deliberately casual tone. One of them said, "In less than forty-eight hours we shall be on the boat at Dubrovnik." They spoke in German. At the sound of the language, Joey gave one of his imperious jerks of the head, which told Stephen to go outside.

"I wonder they've got the nerve to show their faces in this country," Joey said furiously, almost slamming the church door behind him. "What if Granddad and Mr. Mustapha see them?"

"For heaven's sake, you're not saying that they would kill them?" Stephen exclaimed in horror.

"Probably not. But they'd stick a nail in their tires." Joey made a very contemptuous gesture at a white Fiat drawn up outside the church.

"Joey, do you know German?"

"I can read it. I can understand enough to know they were going back from Dubrovnik. They'll probably get the ferry to Ancona. This is an Italian hired car."

He gave the registration letter "I" a light but contemptuous kick.

"Behave yourself, Joey," said Stephen automatically. "Look, I took German in school. Those men aren't German, they're Swiss. I've heard the accent before. It's at least as different from High German as broad Yorkshire is from Scots."

"You're Yorkshire, aren't you?" said Joey, and when

Stephen nodded, he went on, "That, of course, is why I speak English better than you do."

There was some truth in this, for Joey had the barely accented voice of the Highland Scot, which some people say is the purest form of English, but it annoyed Stephen. He was aware of an impulse, which almost shocked him by its intensity, to seize hold of Joey and spank him.

Roger, meanwhile, was happily halfway up a cliff.

He had got on with Stephen much better than he had dared to expect, but nonetheless there was no disguising the fact that Stephen was interested in things to which he himself was frankly indifferent. As for the boy, Joey, Roger considered that he was "too clever by half." It was quite a relief to leave them and to enjoy a little mild rock climbing, which gave a feeling of satisfaction to his mind and to the muscles of arms and legs alike.

He had gone beyond the church and the mosque, and found that the valley grew narrower and the mountains on either side steeper. In places there were outcrops of limestone cliffs, and it was one of those he was busy climbing.

After a while, he decided to go no farther. He was alone, nobody knew where he was, and the limestone was crumbly. All the instructors who had taught him had dinned the need to be sensible into his mind. He wandered a little farther up the valley, and it became narrower still. It was then that he noticed the caves.

The caves were set a little above the base of the cliff, but the ground below was so scattered with fallen rocks that they would be accessible to an active boy or a sure-footed animal. Roger clambered up to one. He had to bend down to enter the cave, but after that the roof arched and he could stand upright. The floor was covered with

44

a litter of dried leaves and bones, and there was a very strong smell. The first word to come into Roger's mind was "Zoo."

Without any conscious thought, he was back out of the cave, and making his way down again. The previous night, he had not really believed Granddad's stories about the bear stealing his grapes. But what was it that lived in the cave?

He approached the next cave, which was much harder to get to, with a great deal of caution. The entrance was higher, but even so he stood and sniffed carefully. There was nothing worse than stale air. He went in, and then stood patiently for his eyes to adjust to the darkness. When he came out, he was feeling very puzzled. He stood on a ledge by the mouth of the cave, and Stephen and Joey, who came walking along the road below at that moment, could tell from his attitude that something unexpected had happened.

"Roger," called Stephen. "What have you found up there?"

Roger stared down, surprised to see them.

"Come and have a look."

"How?"

"How? Oh, I'll get down and show you if you really can't see."

Roger was prepared to admit that what was for him no more than a routine scramble might, for some other people, present a problem. Nonetheless, he felt rather impatient when Stephen, having the footholds pointed out to him, was slow to climb up. Joey, being thin and agile, managed much better. Then they too went into the cave and stood blinking at the darkness after the sunlight.

Stephen's first reaction was an odd feeling that they

were not alone. There were several men standing waiting for them. When he tried to focus them clearly, they disappeared. A moment later they started to swim back into his vision again.

There was a row of figures, the same height as himself, standing as if in procession around the walls of the cave. They were dressed in long white robes, with some other shorter garment draped over, and in the light that filtered in from outside it was possible to see that this was covered with a pattern of crosses. They were faint, insubstantial, like a procession of ghosts.

Joey was carefully feeling the walls of the cave. Instead of having the sharpness and coldness of stone they were smooth to the touch.

"Plaster," he said, half to himself. "As in the churches. You put it on and you paint while it is still wet. So the paint sinks right in, and it lasts for hundreds of years."

"There's more of them," said Roger, looking upward almost uneasily. "Or at least I think so. I wish I had brought a flashlight. We've got one in the car."

Above them, the shapes were more shadowy still. There seemed to be a figure stretched out, with other faces clustered, peering above it. In that dim light it was hard to tell if it was very near to them or far away.

"I think it is the Death of the Virgin," said Joey.

Even as he spoke, by some trick of the light the figures became still fainter, and other faces came into view. They were surrounded not by bodies, but only by clusters of wings.

For a moment there was an illusion that the air itself was vibrating with wingbeats. Then, puzzled and almost a little uneasy, they went out into the daylight again.

46

5

"Mind you," said Roger, as they made their way back to the farm for dinner, "I don't think much of them as paintings. All stiff and unnatural and staring at you. Still, I suppose the people who did them couldn't paint any better."

Joey seemed to be on the brink of a classic explosion of temper, so Stephen said hastily, "It's a particular style of painting, called Byzantine. I think you have to become used to it before it starts making much sense." To his own surprise he added, "I suspect if you really understood it, it might make most other kinds of painting seem rather unsatisfactory."

They questioned Joey's mother about the cave, but she could tell them nothing. Neither could Granddad, except to explain, with a wealth of gestures, that he himself had gone climbing as a boy and nearly been badly hurt when a part of the cliff had broken.

"So do be careful," said Mrs. MacLeod. "Why don't you go to the monastery and ask the abbot about these

47

paintings? He'd be glad to see Roger and Stephen. He was a liaison officer during the war between the partisans and the British military mission. And you could ask Petar as well; after all, he's the expert. He's writing a book on Byzantine icons in Yugoslavia, and he's staying at the monastery guesthouse," she explained to the boys.

Joey looked very mulish at the mention of Petar's name, so his mother said something in Serbian. Joey answered in the same language, and then finally shrugged, as if in resignation. He said, "Very well. I'd like Stephen to see the monastery, in any case. I warn you, though, it can be a bit overwhelming. The abbot of the Bogorodica Monastery used to be a very important person, just as a bishop was at one time in England, and this particular abbot has a highly developed sense of the dignity of his position. And then there is Petar, of course. He may be an art expert, but he's also a six-foot-six Montenegrin, and Montenegrins are ten times as fierce as most other Yugoslavs."

"Do they get on together?" asked Stephen, trying to envisage someone ten times as fierce as Granddad.

"Most of the time. They tend to get together and deplore the fact that I don't treat either of them with as much respect as they think they deserve. But there was rather a lot of friction last week. I only came in on the end of it, and neither of them would tell me the whole story, but it seems that something valuable has been missing for simply ages. Petar said that if the monks weren't such muddlers they'd have found it long ago. So the abbot said that what was meant to be found would be found, and they ended up having a very philosophical row about fate and destiny. Typically Slav," said Joey, his Scottish accent becoming much more noticeable.

They set out in the car, which was fit to use in the daylight, to the Bogorodica Monastery, the name of which Stephen interpreted as meaning "Monastery of the Mother of God." Roger, who was driving, soon wondered where they were going. The valley narrowed until they seemed to be headed straight for an unbroken wall of sheer mountain. The dirt track led them between jagged hunks of rock, each the size of a large house. Just as it seemed to come to a dead end, it twisted sharply, and they entered a very narrow gorge where the wall of mountain had simply been sliced in two. It was so high that, from inside the car, they could not see the sky. Within what seemed inches of the road, a fierce mountain stream pushed its way through the gorge.

Stephen looked around, almost in disbelief.

"Is there really a road through here?"

"There's a road of sorts," said Joey. "It used to be only a goat track. This is the start of the Kurnovo gorge. It goes on for miles like this. In 1916 a large part of our army, including, I need hardly tell you, Granddad and Mr. Mustapha, retreated through this gorge in the depths of winter. When the first men went through, the snow was up over their heads, and they had to force a way through it. By the time the last men came, they were trampling over the bodies of men who had frozen to death. And all the monks of the Bogorodica Monastery went with them as well, carrying the icons and sacred relics and chanting."

"What happened then?" asked Roger. He had no interest at all in Yugoslav history, but as he looked at the gorge, so bleak even in the height of summer, he found himself stirred by the bravery of those men.

"They struggled down to the coast in the end. Then

49

a lot of them died of typhus. The survivors fought their way back from across the Greek border."

"But surely this isn't the only road to the coast?" said Stephen. "I thought I saw another one on the road sign at the crossroads where we bumped one another."

"Yes, that's the new road. They started building it a few years ago, and they're still working on the last section. You can be held up by blasting or by machinery being moved, but, even so, everyone uses it rather than this."

"Do you blame them?" said Roger with feeling, as he edged his way around boulders and over potholes.

Then the gorge widened out into an enclosed valley. They drew up by a high blank wall and went through a huge wooden gate painted yellow ocher, with heavy iron studs all over it. Just inside was a water spout over a trough, and Joey paused to drink. The two older boys meanwhile looked at each other in some surprise. When Joey had talked of a monastery, and of the abbot as an important churchman, they had been expecting something large and impressive. Being English, they had thought of York Minster, of the fortresslike mass of Durham, of the graceful, spreading buildings of Fountains Abbey. This place was tiny in comparison, and it looked more like a farm.

The monastery precincts were surrounded by high buildings, the backs of which, without any windows, formed the wall. They were built in stone with big wooden balconies under projecting eaves. One of the buildings was a barn, with a high, beamed wooden roof, and bunches of onions and herbs hung up to dry. A cock strutted up the barn steps. On the cobbled path in front of them, a peahen tenderly escorted her five small chicks.

At one point, there was a bright splash of flowers, with some wooden beehives set among them. The only thing that showed it was a monastery was the church in the center.

This was distinctly smaller than the average English parish church. It was very much lower, having no spire or tower, but a series of domes bubbling out all over the top. It was built of rough, sunbaked brick, nearer gold than red in color, and roofed with curved tiles that were rather more red than gold. The brick was not laid in straight lines, but in elaborate patterns that followed the shape of the building. It was at the same time simple and intricate, like the seed head of a flower.

Sunning themselves on the roof, with an air of knowing how magnificent they looked, were three large peacocks.

"This way," said Joey, and they went in to a large entrance porch that ran the width of the church. Once again, every inch was covered with paintings, and the first picture they saw looked like a portrait of Joey himself.

He was dressed as a Roman soldier and carried a flaming sword. A golden light blazed around his head, and wings swept over his shoulders. On his face was exactly the expression that Joey wore when he was excited.

"It's the Archangel Michael, actually," said Joey, grinning at their surprise. "Painted about 1300. Petar is putting a picture of me in his book, to show how local types survive. The painting is probably based on one of my ancestors in the valley."

A nun came clucking toward them, dressed in shabby black. She exclaimed with disapproval at Joey's jeans, while apparently accepting the same dress from the two foreign boys.

51

"What's a nun doing here?" whispered Stephen, and Joey hissed back, "We have unisex monasteries here." They went on into the church.

Once again, it was very dark inside, but because a service was taking place, it was illuminated by candles. They flickered on the icons that formed a screen right across the church, making the gold backgrounds shine. A huge circle of candles hung from the central dome. It picked up details of the paintings with which the church was covered, so that there was a feeling of hundreds of half-seen presences joining in the service. The domes of the church were smoke-blackened and in darkness; there, all was mystery.

The main part of the service was taking place behind the screen of the iconostasis. Occasionally, a central door was flung open, revealing a man's figure in silhouette against a bright blaze of candles. A few monks were chanting, and one swung a censer, so that trails of incense lay on the air already thick with candle smoke. An old woman lay prostrate in front of an icon. Two others were having a lively conversation, as if they had just met at a supermarket checkout.

The circle of candles started to sway, and as the light flickered over the walls, face after face flashed kaleidoscopically out of the darkness.

The movement, the lights, the chanting, and the incense were starting to have a faintly hypnotic effect, almost, thought Stephen, as lights and music may do at a disco. Even Roger was a little affected, though he contented himself with muttering, "School prayers were never like this."

At last the service was over, and the light behind the iconostasis dimmed. A man somewhat shorter than Roger, in a long black robe, came striding out. In spite of his monk's garments he walked very vigorously and in the manner of someone used to command. He saw them, and exclaimed "Joey!" in tones of mingled affection and exasperation. Joey said something in Serbian, and the abbot shook his head. Then, speaking in English, Joey introduced Roger and Stephen. The abbot looked steadily at them, and then, as if remembering English from a long time ago in the past, he said gravely, "Welcome." He motioned them to follow him outside.

By contrast with the church, the sunlight was very warm and bright. The abbot sat himself down on a low stone wall. There was something a little bull-like about him, with his fleshy nose, and his long hair and beard forming tight, black curls, that were now going a little gray. Stephen felt, without quite knowing why, that he was not an especially spiritual man, but he was a powerful one.

The abbot turned to Joey.

"Petar is not here. He went off to Skopje last night and comes back this evening. If you ask me, it was to get away from you tormenting him."

A faint look of triumph came over Joey's face, then he said, "In any case, you may be able to help us more than Petar. Did you know there are paintings in one of the caves in the valley?"

"There are paintings in quite a number of caves," said the abbot calmly, and smiled a little maliciously at the look of amazement on Joey's face. "A long time ago, those caves were inhabited, by hermits attached to the monastery. It is all in the manuscript "Chronicle of the Monastery," which has never been published. Then when the Turks came, the hermits stopped living there. The only safe place to lead the religious life was inside the fortified walls of the monastery. The Turks never came in. They tried once, and a stone fell on the head of their leader and killed him."

"Now, I wonder if that was an accident," said Roger almost inaudibly.

"But how did they get to the caves, and get food up, and so on?" asked Stephen.

He stopped to stare at two figures who had just entered the monastery precincts. It was the two men, Swiss-German or whatever they were, whom he and Joey had seen in the little church of Sveti Marko. As he watched, they went into the monastery church. He realized that the abbot was speaking.

"They would have used ladders. It was not quite as dramatic as some of the Greek rock monasteries, where they used to haul visitors up in baskets. There were still the remains of ladders to one or two of the caves when the two English ladies came here just over a hundred years ago."

"The English ladies?" said Roger.

"Or maybe one was Scottish. Joey here always tells me that English and Scottish are different. They came to our country with the idea of founding schools for Christian girls under Turkish rule. Why, I am not quite certain, because at that time there were not many schools for Christian girls in England. But they were two very brave ladies, without any doubt. When they saw the remains of these ladders, they insisted on climbing up, greatly to the alarm of the monks and their mule drivers.

"Then they wrote a book all about their adventures. There used to be a copy which they gave to the monastery. I do not know if we still have it. I looked at it once. They mentioned the paintings in some of the caves, which is how I happen to know about them. I am glad you reminded me. I shall have a look for the book, and Petar can go and inspect the paintings."

"Only we shall go first," said Joey, with considerable determination.

"Tell me," said Roger, and paused, completely uncertain of how to address a dignitary of the Serbian Orthodox Church. "Would these hermits have lived in the caves all the time, sir?"

"Oh, yes. I have lived in a cave myself. It was not really much colder than my cell in the monastery here."

The abbot's tone was very matter-of-fact. As he spoke, his hands, which had been folded inside his sleeves, came out, and he made a quite involuntary gesture with his fingers. Roger recognized it as the movement a man makes with a gun.

"You mean when you fought with the Partisans, sir?"

"Yes, when I was about your age. I had been two years in the monastery, but not yet taken my final vows. We had no money to spare for clothes, so I cut the long skirt off my habit, and fought with a gun in my hands and a cross around my neck.

"And now I am the abbot of the Bogorodica Monastery, and I fight to keep my faith and my monastery alive in a Communist country. This, Joey, is the answer to what you are longing to ask me—why I have never gone treasure hunting in caves. I have so much else to think of.

"But you three go and see what you can find, and come back and tell me. Then, when Petar returns from Skopje, he can go and look too."

He hesitated, as if he were about to say something more, when he noticed that the nun, who seemed to act

55

as a general servant to the monastery, was hovering around them. She spoke to him anxiously. The abbot raised his hand in dismissal and strode off after her to the church.

"It's those tourists," explained Joey. "There's a sign forbidding photographs, and they simply ignored it."

"Camera maniacs," Stephen said. "I wouldn't have thought that anyone could have wanted as many pictures as they were taking in Sveti Marko."

"I don't envy them getting the rough side of the abbot's tongue," put in Roger. "He's rather formidable."

It was, Stephen acknowledged, an apt word for this warrior-priest. He suddenly found himself wondering just what it was that the abbot really believed in.

6

As they drove farther up the valley, the sides of the gorge closed in again and the road surfaces became even worse. A bend in the road took them out of sight of the monastery, and Roger stopped the car. There was just room to park on a rocky patch of ground overlooking the turbulent river, which here had a strange, metallic-green color. On either side of them, the cliffs rose up sheerly, so steep that they could see the sky only by craning their heads right backward. There was a chill, as if the sun never reached here, and the sound of the river made an almost deafening echo in that confined space.

"There are plenty of caves," said Roger, staring up at the cliffs, which were pockmarked with round holes. "It's an absolute gamble. We could strike something with the first one, or look at dozens for nothing."

"Forget the other side of the river. You'd never get across," said Stephen. He stared down at the water, which battered its way around and between the rocks.

"When our army retreated in 1916, there weren't any bridges," said Joey. "They had to wade through the water, and many of them were drowned."

It was almost obsessional, thought Stephen, this feeling that Joey had for his country and what it had suffered. Yet, from what his mother had told them, he had an equal fanaticism in his feeling for Scotland. Probably these almost excessively strong feelings spilled over into his relationships with other people. What had Mrs. Mac-Leod and the abbot been hinting at about this art historian from Belgrade? What could he be to Joey, or Joey to him? There was something oddly disconcerting about the boy, which might simply be his own tensions communicating themselves to other people.

Meanwhile Roger, happily free of tensions, was halfway up a cliff.

"I hope to goodness the rock is firm," said Joey, as if heroic death on the grand scale were something to be admired, but the prospect of Roger's falling and spraining his ankle were a far more serious matter.

"He knows what he's doing," said Stephen defensively, and they watched Roger carefully test a tree growing out of a crack in the rock to see if it would take his weight.

Roger ignored them. He was absorbed in climbing. He, who had found work at school mainly something to be endured, felt a positive mental excitement in looking for handholds and footholds.

It was, he felt, a very easy climb, compared to many that he had done, for the surface of the stone was pitted and fissured all over. It was different from any English limestone that he had seen, being much whiter in color, and his doubt lay in wondering how firm it was. He tested each hold deliberately before shifting his weight. If he did slip, there was no one to save him, because he was climbing alone. He wished he had someone who shared his own tastes. There would be little future in trying to teach Stephen to climb. As Stephen's driving showed at times, his coordination between body and brain was well short of perfect.

He wondered about Joey as a companion. Joey was undoubtedly agile, but Roger felt that he had no wish, when halfway up a mountain, to be subjected to a harangue on how somebody he had never heard of had won some battle or other. In any case, he reflected, half echoing Stephen, in some strange way one was always too much aware of Joey. He had never met so young a boy who could make one so conscious of his presence. So thinking, he hauled himself over a very sharp ledge of rock and crawled into the first cave on his hands and knees.

The floor was covered with fallen stone and a few scraps of dead vegetation blown in by the wind. Otherwise, there was nothing at all. Roger called down to Stephen and Joey, who were standing by the foot of the cliff, talking earnestly to one another, and then turned to the slight problem of how to get out of the cave and back onto the face of the cliff.

The next cave he explored was just as empty. At this point, Roger felt very tempted to give up, but sounds from below told him that Stephen and Joey were having an argument about Scottish nationalism. Stephen, for long accustomed to having things all his own way in debates at school, seemed to have met his match. Exhausting brat, Joey, thought Roger, and turned to the more congenial task of taking his afternoon walk on a nearly vertical cliff face.

The third cave was mildly more interesting in that it had a crack in the rock through which, in winter, water seeped from above. There was a channel, now dry, which suggested that at times a waterfall must come pouring out of the cave. He wondered whether he should climb down, but gathering from the voices below that they were now on the subject of offshore oil rights, he decided to stay where he was. He noticed another cave, a little farther along the cliff and some twenty feet from the ground.

It was easier to get to from above, where Roger was, than it would have been from below, for at this point, the cliff overhung its base by several feet. There was what looked like a firm ledge of rock jutting out from the mouth of the cave. Roger worked his way along toward it, carefully considering how he would find a route back. At last, he stood on the ledge.

What was it the abbot had said about ladders, and even hauling people up in baskets? Of all the caves he had seen, this one would have been the easiest to have put a ladder up to. Unfortunately, he could not look in, for the mouth was blocked by a stone. It was unusually neatly blocked, thought Roger, and with the first stirrings of excitement he started to try to push the stone out of the way.

After several minutes, he had got nowhere at all. This might have been the end, for Roger had no very great interest in what was in the cave, but he did have a temperamental dislike for being defeated. He pushed again, and this time he managed to move the stone so that he could wriggle in.

He smelled the cold dry air of the cave, and he saw bare rock. This was obviously no hermit's chapel, such as the cave they had seen that morning had been. There was nothing here except for fragments of stone on the floor, which shifted beneath his feet. He shone the small flashlight which, in view of the morning's find, he had taken from their camping equipment. The cave went up in a funnel shape over his head. He flashed the light at random around the walls, which were dull and blank. He had had enough. His hand moved the light, but his mind was not paying attention. The light shone into a little niche, oddly like that empty niche in the living room at the farmhouse. He stared up at it without any real interest, and what looked like a woman with a black face stared fixedly back at him.

Meanwhile the two tourists, who were, of course, Klaus and Heinrich, were getting the "rough side of the abbot's tongue," and as Roger had surmised, it was not an especially pleasant experience. As abbot of the Bogorodica Monastery he spoke as a prince of the Church; as an ex-Partisan he spoke with a still-living hatred of Germans. He was also, it must be admitted, a human being who was rather fond of the sound of his own voice.

Klaus and Heinrich decided, wisely, that it was useless to argue. Nevertheless there was one point they wanted to put straight.

"We are not Germans," said Klaus in English, the language which they had ended up speaking. "We come from Switzerland. *Schweiz. Svizzera. Suisse.*"

"Swizzerland," said the abbot, and a faint smile appeared among the fronds of his beard. He knew that the Swiss were a neutral people, and to one of his temperament neutrality was very hard to imagine. He also knew they were wealthy, and that much of the world's riches lay in vaults beneath the city of Zürich. He thought of the poverty of his once-great monastery.

"Sometimes we do permit photographs in the church. There is, of course, a fee."

"How much?" asked Klaus.

The abbot, in a voice as if the whole question bored him, named a sum ten times greater than what he normally charged. Klaus looked doubtful, then paid it. The abbot inclined his head, and then with intense dignity stalked away.

"Robber!" said Heinrich with feeling. "Who does he think he is? An oil sheikh?"

"I am not quite sure why I paid him," said Klaus, unwilling to admit that something about the abbot had almost hypnotized him into doing so. "Quite obviously, none of the pictures here would ever be any use to us with a man like that around."

"They could give us some ideas, though," said Heinrich, and they started to photograph. An old woman who had come into the church stood there, staring as if in a trance, so that they could not be certain if she was aware of what they were doing or not. Then the fussy nun came in with a broom rather like a witch's broom and started to sweep the floor in an unsystematic way, leaving little piles of dust as she went. Heinrich gazed up at a fresco of the Agony in the Garden. The somber colors with strong highlights, and the attitudes of the figures, frozen in anguish, gave it a tremendous feeling of power.

The nun saw him looking, and something in his obvious admiration moved her. She muttered at him. Heinrich, still rapt by the paintings, paid no attention, but Klaus came to listen.

"I think she's trying to speak English. And if I've got it right, she's telling us that the abbot says there are more paintings somewhere."

The nun chattered on.

"I can't make it out," Klaus said at last. "But suppose we drive on a little way up the valley."

After the first moment of shock, Roger realized that it was only a picture. He reached up for it. Although it was not very big, a bit less than two feet wide and rather more in height, it was surprisingly heavy, being painted on a solid panel of wood as thick as a door. He carried it into the daylight.

"Here," he shouted. "I've got something. Another of these stiff, staring pictures. It's a Madonna and child, I think, and they both seem to have black faces. Could you catch it if I chuck it down?"

"For goodness' sake, don't," screamed Joey. "Think of the damage."

"Do you think it's worth anything?"

"I've no idea, never having seen it," said Stephen. "But I do know that Russian icons, which look very much like a lot of paintings here, have sold for over ten thousand pounds."

Roger looked at the icon in honest surprise.

"What I need is a rope to lower it down. Shall I leave it here, and we'll go back and get something?"

Stephen moved to the car, but Joey said, "Wait," and began to unwind the bulky cummerbund he wore around his waist underneath his jerkin. To their surprise it consisted of yard after yard after yard of flat brown cord.

"What an extraordinary costume," said Stephen. "That is, I hope you don't mind my saying so."

"It's a genuine nineteenth-century national costume," said Joey, still busy unwinding. "Most of the time I live in a T-shirt and jeans like you two. Then, the other day, I found this in a chest at home. It belonged to some ancestor. I tried it on, and when I found that it fitted, I thought I might as well wear it. After all, this is one of the few parts of Europe where most people still wear national costume as a matter of course. But I didn't put on the bottom half. It was much too hot and constricting."

"But what's the idea of all the rope?" asked Stephen, starting to coil it.

"Protective clothing. The Turks enjoyed kicking Christians, and they used to aim at the kidneys. This absorbed some of the blow."

Joey took the rope, and flung it toward Roger. It fell far short, and began to uncoil.

"Oh, give me," said Stephen impatiently.

"You're as bad as a pair of girls," said Roger a moment later. At the third attempt, Stephen landed the rope on the ledge. Roger started to tie up the painting, and then looked doubtful.

"What if it gets scratched? Joey, can you spare your genuine antique waistcoat, or whatever it is you are wearing?"

"Yes, but be careful with it. Petar, this man that I told you about, is furious at me for wearing it. He says that the embroidery is much better than modern work, and it ought to be in a museum."

Joey stripped off the loose, jerkin-like garment, which fell to the top of his thighs, and a moment later, it was

64

on the ledge beside Roger. Roger wrapped up the icon, and then, very carefully, started to lower it. It swung clear of the cliff face, and Joey and Stephen stepped out on the narrow cart track in order to catch it.

"Won't be long," muttered Roger. He looked at the brown cord to reassure himself that it was strong enough, and lowered the icon another few feet. "Ready to catch it, you two?"

He peered down on them—on Stephen, scowling a little with concentration, and on Joey, alive and eager, now dressed only in linen shirt and jeans and standing with arms upstretched to receive the icon. Roger stared at Joey with growing amazement.

Then three things happened so close together that Roger could not be certain about the sequence. A car in the road hooted at Joey and Stephen to move. Roger said out loud, "What a fool I've been!" And the ledge of stone on which he was standing started to crumble away.

7

Klaus and Heinrich drove on up the valley. The road surface became worse and worse. The disagreements between the two, and the conflict in character which was always there, came increasingly to the surface.

"It strikes me we are wasting our time," said Heinrich. "I'm not even sure that the old girl really said there are any paintings up here. It isn't the sort of place that one can imagine anyone wanting to live in, let alone have a church."

They looked around the narrow gorge. Even to the two Swiss, used to mountain country, there was something extraordinarily desolate about the sheer, bare cliffs, and the vivid green of the water that cascaded over the rocks.

"There's not much to lose," Klaus said sharply. "So far, we have only found one place in this area that would be any use to us, and that is the little church that we went to before lunch. There are several quite accessible paintings there. The church in Starigrad that we went to after lunch was no use at all—the paintings were all on the walls. As for that monastery, I have every intention of keeping out of the abbot's way. Let's go another mile or two up this road, and then turn around and take the new road to Dubrovnik."

"If you can manage to turn around!" said Heinrich. Klaus, who was driving, edged the car on through a narrow gap between boulders. They came around a bend in the road.

They saw that a car, a small British compact, was parked on a rocky patch of ground between the road and the river. Two boys, their heads craning upward, were blocking the road.

"That's the pair we saw in the little church," said Heinrich, feeling vaguely disturbed for a reason that he could not understand.

"Teenagers all look alike to me," said Klaus. "Nothing but hair and jeans. You can't tell what nationality they are any longer, or even what sex half the time."

"Didn't you look at the redhead? Those eyes and cheekbones come straight from a Byzantine painting."

Heinrich gazed at Joey, who was standing gesticulating in the middle of the road, with fascination. Klaus impatiently honked his horn. Joey, arms stretched upward to catch what was being lowered, shouted something in Serbian that was obviously insulting.

Then came a crash. A huge piece of rock, dislodged from the cliff, hurtled toward the ground. Roger lost his grip on the cord, and the picture that he was lowering came tumbling down. Everyone stood frozen still in horror, and then suddenly acted.

Klaus put the car into reverse, and hastily shot backward. He could not be sure if he had acted in time, or if it was sheer luck that the rock did not hit him as it crashed to the ground.

Instinct made Stephen react. Without being aware that

he had moved, he found himself several feet from the spot where he had been standing. Then the rock fell, and pieces came splintering off. They spattered his face, and for a moment he could not see.

The only one not to jump out of the way was Joey. Some fighting strain, born of his Highland and Yugoslav blood, made him wait long enough to catch hold of the icon. It was much heavier than he had expected. He fell to the ground, still clutching it, and then was covered with stones and dust when the rock fell a few inches away from him.

Roger's reaction was sheer self-preservation. When he felt the ledge of stone on which he was standing begin to crumble, he flung himself backward into the cave. Before he had time to pick himself up, he heard the crash as the rock hit the ground. Only then did he remember that he had let the icon fall.

He made his way cautiously to the mouth of the cave. He assumed that he must have weakened the ledge by all the heaving and pushing that he had done to dislodge the stone that had been blocking the mouth. If so, he must be careful that no more fell. He called, "Stephen, Joey, are you all right?" and was annoyed to find he was breathing so fast from shock that he could not shout loudly. In the end, he crouched there, and peered out.

Because he was out of reach, he felt an extraordinary sense of detachment, as if he were watching something on a television screen and was not involved at all. He saw Stephen bending down with his hands to his eyes, trying desperately to get rid of something that was impeding his sight. He saw Joey, lying flat on the ground, winded, half hidden by the icon.

Then the door of the car was opened, and a man got

out. To Roger from above, he looked vaguely Middle European, rather than Yugoslav, and his clothes gave the impression of a respectable, prosperous citizen. He was obviously doing what any responsible person would do, which was to see whether Joey was really hurt. In order to do so, it was necessary to move the icon. This was still loosely wrapped in Joey's long, woolen jerkin, but the wrapping had slipped and a corner of it was showing. While Roger watched, the man moved the picture, and Joey made a noise halfway between a grunt and a groan.

Roger was just going to shout down, "Are you all right, Joey?" when the man suddenly acted. He lifted the wrapping, took a quick look at the icon, stood still as if in total astonishment, and then seized the icon and began to run clumsily back to the car. He opened a door and flung it onto the back seat. His companion, who had been standing beside the car, stood motionless all this time and stared at him in amazement. The man who had taken the icon shouted, and they both dived into the car.

Roger's feeling of detachment turned into impotent fury.

"Stop it! Stop it!" he shouted. He looked desperately, but he could see no way to get down now that the ledge was broken. Could he jump? It would be more or less like jumping from the roof of an ordinary house, which would have been bad enough with a soft landing, but here he would land among boulders, and probably break his leg. He found he was yelling, "Stephen! Joey!"

The man had started the car again and began to drive forward. Joey was still in the road, now raised to a half-sitting position, but looking extremely confused. There was no room to drive around. Time seemed to stretch out in a terrifying way, so that fractions of seconds felt

69

like minutes as Roger watched the car drive on toward Joey.

Then, just short of him, it stopped. There was no room to turn, for Stephen's car filled the only space left between the road and the river. With a horrible slither of tires on the stones, the Fiat went into reverse. It took an alarming backward course through the boulders.

With the noise of the car, Stephen lifted his face almost blindly. At the same moment, Joey stood up, and then bent double again as if breathing were still painful.

"They've got the picture, and I'm stuck here," Roger said urgently. "For goodness' sake, can't you stop them?"

Stephen rushed automatically to his car. It was pointing up the valley, and so was facing the wrong way. He drove it forward a little, as if preparing to turn it. Roger, once again feeling very detached, noticed how little space he had for maneuvering, with the river rushing so fiercely beside the road. He would not want to turn the car there himself, which meant it might be beyond Stephen's power to do so. Then he realized that there was a further complication. By driving forward, Stephen had put the fallen rocks in between himself and the car he meant to follow. Stephen must have realized this, for he got out and stared at the rock rather blankly. He gave it an experimental push.

Meanwhile, the man who had taken the icon had found a place between river and cliff just wide enough for him to turn his car around. He drove backward and forward, the engine protesting loudly, and managed to gain a few inches each time. The car bounced wildly on the rocky road, and the back door, which he had not shut firmly, burst open.

The first person to realize that this had happened was

Joey. At the sight, he suddenly came back to life again. Roger saw him run, loose linen shirt flapping, toward the car. It had come to a stop for the moment, with a back wheel caught in a particularly deep hole. As the driver roared the engine in an effort to get it out, Joey grabbed the back door handle and flung the door wider open.

Roger nearly fell out of the cave in his effort to see what would happen. He saw Joey stretching across the car, for the icon was on the far side of the back seat. Because of its weight, it would be hard to pull it out in the few seconds available.

"Go on! You're nearly there!" panted Roger.

But, as he spoke, the car passenger woke up to what was happening. He spun around in his seat. Roger assumed the man was trying to seize the icon from Joey, then realized that he had hold of Joey himself. The driver turned around as well, and with a flurry of heels and loud shouts, Joey was dragged into the car. The back door was slammed. Next moment, with a final spatter of stones thrown up by the wheels, the car came out of the pothole, and drove on down the valley. Within a few seconds it disappeared around a bend in the road.

"Go on. *Do* something," shouted Roger. He clenched his fists with exasperation as he saw Stephen stoop down by the river and wash his face in the icy water. It seemed a very long time before Stephen stood up again.

"I can't do anything until I have washed all this grit out of my eyes. While I am doing that, you might get down yourself."

"But I can't. Don't you understand? The foothold I used to get in here has gone, and I'm stuck in this blasted cave. I suppose you are going to tell me that I ought to try to get out by climbing up. Well, for your information, it's only about three thousand feet to the top."

"You mean that you're *stuck?*" said Stephen. He made the words sound like some major discovery, such as finding the law of gravity.

"Give me patience!" said Roger. "Look, I've been working out what we'll have to do. You run down to the monastery and get the abbot. He's the sort of man who would be of some use in an emergency. Meanwhile I will find a way down somehow, and I can probably manage to turn the car. Only you must hurry. It's not the picture that matters. They've got Joey."

"If ever I saw a boy who could look after himself, it was Joey MacLeod," said Stephen.

"You don't understand," started Roger, "that is . . . unless I have gone crazy, and can't believe my eyes."

Stephen, completely ignoring all that Roger had said, got into the car again. He started the engine and drove off, away up the narrow gorge and up into the mountains.

Roger assumed that he had gone in search of a place to turn. He turned his own attention to studying the cliff face and trying to find a way down.

It was several minutes before it occurred to him that Stephen was not coming back.

8

Joey, bewildered, dizzy and out of breath, collapsed onto the back seat of the car, and almost instinctively clutched hold of the icon. A hand reached over the front seat to drag it away. Acting again without any conscious thought, Joey leaned forward and bit the wrist. The hand jerked away, and its owner swore in German.

"What on earth made you take the icon?" he then said to the driver.

The driver was doing his best to go very fast over the bumpy rocks in the road, so he could not turn around to look at Joey, but before answering this question he said in a threatening voice, *"Sprechen Sie Deutsch?"*

"Nein," replied Joey firmly, and settled down to listen to the men's conversation.

Joey, in fact, could read German fairly well, but had much less knowledge of the spoken language than Stephen, and so was able to get only the general gist of what they were saying. Two things emerged very clearly. The driver, the elder man of the two and clearly the

73

leader, had taken the icon on a sudden impulse. He had absolutely no scruples about it, and neither had his companion. It seemed, though, that they had gone against some prearranged plan that they were in Yugoslavia only to spy out the land. What they were spying it out for, Joey could not be certain. They had then gone still further outside their plan by dragging Joey into the car.

Both men became rather agitated, as if they were in a situation entirely new to them. They wanted to get rid of Joey, as quickly as possible, and had no idea of how best to do it at least risk to themselves.

The younger man said, "It would surely be possible to abandon somebody up in those mountains, and they couldn't find help for hours. It's the most godforsaken country I've ever seen."

"But we must give ourselves time to get safely across the border. Really, we need to get back to Milan and hand over this car before anyone starts asking questions. And that is a matter of days, rather than hours."

Any moment now, thought Joey, they will be deciding that the only safe thing is to get rid of me for good. The one advantage I've got is that I don't think they'd be very sure of how to go about it. But the trouble is that this is the sort of country where it would be horribly easy to fake an accident. So what am I going to do?

They had now driven out of the gorge, and were racing down the valley as fast as the bad road surface allowed. Joey, in the back seat, was thrown up and down, and several times bounced right up to the roof of the car. They drove past the mosque, and the farmhouse came into sight.

Now or never, thought Joey. If Mother or Granddad

are around . . . Even the twins would be better than nobody.

There was no one in sight at all.

Next Joey looked at the rocky ground on either side of the road, and tried to calculate how fast they were going. To jump out would mean an odds-on risk of a broken arm or leg.

Well, then, Joey decided, we are more or less bound to go near Starigrad. Let's wait and see if there's anyone there who can help.

The other thing would be to throw the icon out of the car. If somebody comes along the road, even if I don't know them, I will throw the icon out at them and shout to explain. My great advantage is that I speak the language, and I don't believe these men do. Or I could throw the icon out anyhow. After all, it was that they wanted, not me.

If I throw it out, it will probably ruin it. It would serve those men right. The only thing is, I don't know what I'd be ruining.

So, for the first time, Joey tried to look at the icon. They were going too fast on the bumpy road to form any clear impression, except that it seemed very old.

A number of thoughts rushed, confusingly, into Joey's mind together. What was it the abbot had said about the caves not having been used since the Turkish conquest? If the icon had been there all that time, did it mean that it had been painted more than six hundred years ago? Did that make it very valuable? What did "valuable" mean? Money, or something more?

Originally, Joey had acted entirely on impulse, but now for the first time a thought came clearly.

This icon matters. I think it is really worth saving.

They drove past the outskirts of Starigrad. It was now late afternoon, and the summer heat hung heavily over the land. Nobody was around. In another couple of hours, the people would be leaving the fields and their workshops to converge for the evening stroll through the streets of the town. For the moment, the only sign of life was a dog that lay in the dust. Joey saw no chance to act.

They did not go into the town, as Joey had expected, but instead turned on the new road that led to Titograd and Dubrovnik. They were probably heading toward the coast. The question was whether they would, in the lonely mountain country that lay ahead, try to get rid of Joey before they arrived.

Stephen drove on up the valley. He felt rather distressed at abandoning Roger, but Roger, with any luck, could look after himself. The cave was not so very high from the ground, and Roger, after all, was quite an experienced climber. More experienced as a climber than I am as a driver, Stephen thought grimly.

It was unfortunate that he had had no time to explain the plan he had rapidly formed, but he assumed that Roger's own mind might work along the same lines, and that he would guess what was happening. In any case, Stephen realized, he had committed himself to a particular course, and it was already too late to turn back.

As he drove farther, the road became even worse. The gap between the sheer wall of the cliff and the river narrowed until it seemed very little wider than the wheel base of the car. What would happen if he met another car Stephen could not imagine.

To make matters much worse, the river, which up until now had been on the same level as the road, was running through a rocky cleft a long way below. Stephen looked down once and saw a sheer drop to the vivid green water, which was heavily flecked with white foam. He gulped and kept his eyes firmly on the road.

Then he had the feeling, so bewildering, indeed terrifying, to a driver, that he had lost the road. All he could see ahead were two steep walls of rock, far too high to have any visible top, that drew nearer and nearer to one another. They narrowed until they were less than two yards apart. So little daylight came into this crevice that everything was black, except for the clouds of spray thrown up by the stream as it battered its way through.

Stephen braked, and managed to stall the engine. He stared, trying to make some pattern out of what lay ahead. Surely there must be a tunnel? Or rather, he decided, there was a sort of groove hollowed out in the cliff, so that you drove the car under a roof of rock, but were open on one side to a sheer drop. He drove in, and the darkness swallowed him up.

Somewhere inside his head Roger's voice said, "Put your headlights on!"

But where was the headlight switch? Stephen had done no night driving, and so he only knew in theory. He had no instinctive memory in his outstretched hand. In the end, he had to stop the car once again before he could switch on the lights.

Now it was not easy, but at least it was possible to drive on. He kept as close as he could to the inner wall of rock. Then suddenly came a dazzle of light. Was he out in the open again? He blinked, and saw another car facing him a few feet away.

This posed problems so alarming that at first his mind simply rejected the situation. There *can't* be another car, he thought. Then he saw that the other car was slowly starting to back up. Stephen tried to follow and felt his car jerk. What on earth had he done wrong now? Was he in third gear rather than first?

They went on for what seemed like a very long way until they reached daylight. Then the other car tucked itself into a hollowed-out space under the cliff, leaving Stephen to drive on the outer side. He realized that they must have been going uphill in the darkness, for the drop here was farther than ever before. There was no boundary of any sort to the edge of the road, and the ground looked crumbly and insecure.

Stephen was quite convinced that there was no room for his own car to pass.

The other man sat and looked at him, with a grin half sympathetic and half amused.

Stephen shut his eyes, checked his gear lever, and started. He opened his eyes just enough to stare at the side of the other car and at the edge of the road. Then, with an extraordinary sensation of calm, he drove through the narrow gap.

I've done it, he thought. I can do it. And in fact, it's not just me who thinks that this road is appalling. The guidebook calls it one of the worst and one of the most spectacular roads in Europe. If I can do this, I guess that I can do anything.

It then occurred to him that he had been so set on carrying out his scheme that he had missed a possible chance of getting help. He might have tried to ask the man in the other car to take a message to the monastery. It was now too late.

By this time, Roger had managed to clamber down the cliff. It had become obvious that Stephen was not coming back. Roger's feelings veered between alarm and anger. They needed the car in order to get help quickly. What right had Stephen simply to disappear? He also wondered, thinking of what he had heard about the Kurnovo gorge, if the road was not too dangerous for Stephen to drive it safely.

Stephen pressed on with increasing confidence. The road was now climbing rapidly and the gorge became wider, but, at the same time, more winding. He kept coming up to blind corners around the wall of the cliff, and each time he sounded his horn. He met no more traffic, for presumably everyone who could do so was using the new road.

The new road was the basis of the plan that Stephen had made. When Joey was captured, he had had to decide very quickly what he should do. He knew that he could never drive fast enough to catch up with the more powerful Fiat. The men had talked of going to Dubrovnik to board the ferry for Italy. In that case, they would almost certainly take the new road to the coast.

But Stephen, who had studied the map the previous night, had noticed that the old road was much shorter in distance. When he found that he could not turn the car around, he had decided to gamble and take the old road. With any luck, he should arrive first at the place where the two roads converged, which was high up in the mountains, very near to the Yugoslav-Albanian border.

As to what he would actually do when the other car came, he had no idea.

His plan had been partly based on the assumption that Roger would guess what he had in mind. Unfortunately,

Roger had never looked carefully at this particular map. Stephen also assumed, in this case rightly, that Roger would manage to climb down from the cave, and would hasten to look for help.

Roger found himself outside the heavy gates of the Bogorodica Monastery, which looked like half farm, half fortress. He hurried in, and the peahen, sensing his urgency, shooed her brood of chicks out of his way.

He was met this time by a young monk with a pale face. Roger asked for the abbot, and the young monk, half understanding, shook his head. He managed somehow to convey that the abbot had left on a visit to some other monastery. Roger thought that it might be a place called Pec. He could not discover when he was coming back.

Once again, the fussy nun came hurrying up, anxious to show that she understood a little English. The trouble was that her English was harder for Roger to follow than the young man's Serbian. He thanked them both, and with some little difficulty escaped, then hurried off down the valley in search of Joey's mother. Although normally Roger's impulse would have been to turn to one of his own sex, he had an impression, based on no rational knowledge at all, that Joey's mother had, in her time, dealt with even worse situations.

He was feeling more shaken than he liked to admit by his very narrow escape when the ledge of rock had broken, and so he found it hard to order his thoughts. All he could do was to wonder if he would ever see Joey again.

It would not have been true to say that Stephen was

enjoying himself, but he did have the feeling of stimulus that comes from reacting to a challenge. One challenge was that of the road itself, and of finding that he could increasingly work out how to take the car around each bend. The other challenge was that of the need to keep going, to do as fast a time on the bad road as the more powerful car would do on the good. Otherwise, he would gain nothing by doing the shorter distance.

Once, his nerve nearly failed him completely.

He was climbing all the time, and the tops of the cliffs now seemed only hundreds, rather than thousands, of feet above. More and more sky came into view.

From some distance he had been aware of a flimsy bridge ahead that was slung across a narrow point of the gorge. It flashed in and out of his sight as he drove around bends. The look of the bridge, slung hundreds of feet above the riverbed, reminded him of pictures that he had seen of primitive suspension bridges in the high Andes. It must be there for shepherds to bring their sheep and goats down from the mountains.

Of course, no one could drive a car over it, thought Stephen, trying hard to suppress his fear that that was exactly what he was going to do. But it was rather sinister that the road seemed to continue from the other side of the bridge. That must mean that the bridge would look much more substantial when you actually came close to it.

It looked much more frail.

Originally, thought Stephen, the bridge had been made of planks slung on ropes. The ropes had been reinforced by steel cables, but the planks remained. The whole structure swayed slightly in the air. He looked down, but it was almost too dark to make out the river so far below.

It was simply not reasonable. Such things did not belong to the modern world. But did the market at Starigrad belong to the modern world? Did the monastery, with its flickering lights and its incense, and that multitude of faces peering down from its walls? Did the twin Muslim girls, hiding behind their veils, or the two old men who spoke of killing as other men spoke of playing cards? It was he and his car which were out of place. They were the intruders in this strange country, where even earth and water seemed to express an intensity of emotion.

Would the bridge bear the weight of the car?

Was it safer to drive over slowly, or very quickly?

If Stephen had been asked the previous day if he would crawl over that bridge on his hands and knees, he would have answered No.

So he drove the car across it, and with every turn of the wheels, the bridge swayed more and more.

After that, it was better.

The road climbed gradually to upland, twisting around a succession of hairpin bends. Now, instead of bare rocks, there was sparse scrubby pasture by the side of the road, but still there was always the drop on the other side. Stephen began to relax a little.

But even had he been concentrating, he would have had no warning of what happened next. The many miles over flint-sharp stones had weakened one of the tires. Quite suddenly, it burst.

Stephen had no experience of what to do in a skid. His life was at stake. The car slithered helplessly on small stones, and then started to tilt. Stephen saw down into the valley below as if from a banking airplane. He knew that there was no barrier at the edge to restrain him.

He waited for blackness to rise up and overwhelm him.

9

From the moment that they left Starigrad, Joey's
chance of escape went down steeply. Soon they were
running through hilly country that was covered with
trees—oaks and beeches of an extraordinary height. It was
very green for somewhere so hot, almost like a piece of
English countryside on a larger scale, and only the pungent, aromatic smell of the undergrowth revealed how
far south they were. There was no one around who might
help.

Joey stared at the icon, and saw a painting of the Virgin,
her head bent over her child. The attitude of the woman's
head and the folds of her mantle were protective and
brooding. For a picture with so little movement, it was
unexpectedly powerful. This much Joey could understand, and that was almost the limit of it. It was hard,
on such a basis, to decide if the icon was worth taking
a risk for, a risk that might even amount to staking one's
own life.

If Joey's friend, Petar Metkovic, had been there, he

would have observed very much more. He would have known that the icon was some seven hundred years old, and had been painted at a time when the artists of that area surpassed those of Italy. He could have said this confidently on technical grounds, but also because of a certain harshness of vision about it, in contrast to the more sentimental style of some later paintings. The mother knew that not even her love could save her son from a horrible death on the cross, and the child himself, who gazed up at her with an alert, unchildlike expression, was already a little aware of what lay ahead.

Petar would also have said that the icon was in amazingly good condition for a painting of such an age that had lain neglected for so long. The coloring of the skin tones had faded a little, revealing the dark-colored background, and this had helped to produce the black effect that had so perplexed Roger. The other factor that had produced the blackness was the smoke of countless candles that had once been burned in front of the icon. The only part that was actually damaged was the bottom edge, where most of the paint had been worn away by the lips of the many worshipers who had kissed it.

Petar would have regretted this damage, since his aim in life was to keep works of art in as good condition as possible, and to display them properly. Joey took an entirely different view. To him the worn patch was a reminder that once the icon had been looked on as something immensely precious.

They were now climbing steadily, as they made their way over the first of the mountain ranges that lay between them and the coast. Although they were on a highway, there was, by the standards of any Western European country, remarkably little traffic. Joey, who had been hoping for some delay in which it might be possible to scramble out of the car with the picture, was alarmed to find how deserted the road was. For the first time, the idea that something very unpleasant might happen up in those lonely mountains became not just a vague prospect but a reality.

Then suddenly came the noise of a car honking from behind. Joey stiffened. Did this mean that Roger and Stephen had managed to come in pursuit? Joey felt for the door handle, but the driver, catching sight of the movement in his mirror, exclaimed angrily, and the younger man turned around to see what was happening. Joey sat very still, and tried to look quite unperturbed. The pursuing car came out to overtake.

It was a Mercedes, and at the wheel was a stranger. Joey went limp with disappointment, then suddenly tensed again. They were driving on the outer side of the road, and there was no barrier, not even stones, between them and a very steep slope. With angry hoots, the Mercedes pushed them over to the very edge of the road. They were approaching a corner. If we go over the edge, I may get out of the car, thought Joey. And a lot of use that is going to be if I'm dead!

The Mercedes shot past them, with a rush of air that made the smaller Fiat shake. The next moment, it had flicked around the corner, the last sight of it being the "D," which Joey knew stood for "Germany," on the license plate.

"The Germans are uncivilized swine," said the younger man, in German.

Stephen could be right, thought Joey, and these two are Swiss. Maybe that's something. The Swiss, on the whole, don't go in for violent crime. I am probably better off with these two than I would be with a couple of former SS men.

It was a limited comfort.

The road wound on and on uphill. Though it was undoubtedly a very much better road than the one that Stephen was taking, it was still steep, twisting, and narrow. As they climbed, there were fewer trees, and more bare walls of rock. The surface, which until then had been tarred, suddenly deteriorated. They had reached the section of road that had not been completed.

Once again, Joey felt hopeful. Where there were road-works, there must be workmen. It might be possible to attract someone's attention. They drove around a bend and came in sight of a man with a red flag.

He was leaning against a large rock in an apparently trancelike state. It must have been some time since the last car, the German one, had gone through, and he obviously was not expecting another. The red flag drooped limply in one hand, and in the other hand, arm outstretched, he held a length of rope that was smoldering slowly.

Joey was the first to realize the significance of it.

"Stop! They're blasting! Don't you see? That rope is the same length as the fuse, and when it's burned through, the explosion comes."

But even as Joey spoke, they drove on past the man. He suddenly realized what had happened and ran to the middle of the road, waving his arms, and shouting wildly after them. Three or four other men, who had been lying talking in the shadow of a big rock, got to their feet and started to run after the car.

The driver raised his hand contemptuously at them, and drove as fast as he could over the stony ground. On one side, the land fell away abruptly. On the other, it sloped upward more gently. Then they came to a blind corner, where the road became very narrow because of a large rock jutting out. Joey suddenly realized that it was probably this piece of rock that was being blasted away.

"For God's sake, stop!" shrieked Joey.

The driver let the steering wheel wobble a little, as if he had only just registered, with surprise, that Joey was speaking English. Then he changed gear and prepared to drive around the corner.

They could feel the earth tremble before they heard the noise of the explosion.

Stephen knew nothing, nothing except for a roaring in his ears, and the pulsing of what seemed like waves coming up to drown him.

He could not move.

After some unknown length of time he realized that the surge and rushing noise were no more than the very violent thudding of his own heart and the blood running through his veins. The reason why he could not move was that his muscles were locked with tension: one leg was stretched out to jam on the foot brake, and the other hand was clutching the hand brake so tightly that sweat dripped visibly off his wrist.

If he let go, would the hand brake still hold the car?

He tried to relax his grip a little, and stared out through the windshield. Ahead of him, he saw nothing but sky. He looked through the driver's window, and once again was aware only of empty space. But through the passenger window was the reassuring sight of solid, rocky ground.

He must get out through the passenger door, but would

87

his movement cause the car to slip over the edge? His brain told him he ought to try, his muscles were reluctant to unlock themselves. Slowly, he moved his foot from the brake, and then, inch by inch, wriggled under the steering wheel. At long last, he reached the door. He must not jolt it in opening it.

He had no recollection of getting out of the car, but when he turned to look at it, and saw how close the front wheel on the driver's side was to the edge of the drop, he turned aside, and was violently and painfully sick.

When he had finished, he had a headache and a horrible taste in his mouth, but the mountain air was sweet and fresh, and at least he was alive.

All around him stretched miles of stony mountainside, so bare that they had the quality of a giant sculpture. The only things that seemed to be alive were the clouds that raced one another, casting huge shadows on the expanse of stone. It was desolate, but on a heroic scale. No wonder that such a place could breed an army that would march on foot through the pass that he had just driven, rather than ever surrender.

The strain and the shock of his narrow escape had left Stephen feeling oddly exalted. In some way, the bare mountainside and racing clouds were all part of the same experience as the dark church, the chanting of monks, and the flickering of candles on the gold icons. Until that day, Stephen had studied Russian at school because he was clever at languages and Russian was a useful one to know. But studying it had made him far more receptive than he was aware to the impact of Eastern Europe. In the last two days he had fallen under the spell of the Slav people, and of the last faint echoes of Byzantium.

His conscious mind told him that he had to change

the wheel, and had already wasted more time than he could afford to.

Fortunately Roger had bullied Stephen into changing a wheel for practice, so that at least he knew what to do. He seized one of the many large stones that lay about, and wedged it under the passenger front wheel. The tire that had gone was the rear one on the driver's side. Acting almost mechanically, and with a degree of calm that surprised him, he managed to change the wheel. This action, so routine to someone like Roger, gave him an enormous sense of achievement.

Then he looked at the stony ground that served as a road. If he went straight backward for a couple of yards, he could then start to turn. He sat in the car, and his heart started thumping again. All would be well if he was really in reverse, but he was not very good at finding reverse.

When he was almost, almost certain that he was in the right gear, he drove slowly off. A moment later, he was again on his way.

He had lost so much time that it became a gamble as to whether or not he would reach the place where the roads linked up before the other car did so. Now, for the first time, he began to wonder. Assuming that he got there first, what on earth was he going to do?

10

An inexperienced driver, such as Stephen, would have braked at the first impact of the explosion. Klaus reacted more wisely. He jammed his foot down on the accelerator, clutched the steering wheel tightly, and tried to drive out of trouble.

As the car shot forward, the rock, which had been rising into the air, began to fall down again. Just in time, the car passed underneath. When the main mass of falling stone hit the ground, it was already a few yards ahead. Klaus exclaimed with relief. The next moment, the car began to swerve violently and came to an abrupt stop.

"What's happened?" exclaimed Heinrich, but even as he spoke, he saw that the windshield had shattered. Although they had missed the main impact of the explosion, a small fragment of falling rock must have hit it. Angrily, Klaus began to push the rest of the windshield out, and swore when he nicked his fist on a splinter of broken glass.

"I think the car's all right," he muttered.

"Yes, only where is our passenger?" said Heinrich, turning around and staring at the back seat. It was empty.

Klaus got out of the car and looked over the edge of the road. It was too steep for anyone to have climbed down, let alone be hidden there. Behind them on the narrow road was nothing but a cloud of dust, spattered with still falling stones.

"Anyone who walked into that was probably killed," said Heinrich. "We'll have to wait till it settles."

Then, from some distance away, they heard the sound of voices. The road men were coming to see if the explosion had removed enough rock.

"Come on," Klaus said urgently. "We can't stay here."

"How about the icon?" said Heinrich. "That's gone as well."

"In that case, it is probably smashed. But if that confounded kid has been killed, we had better get out of the way. We'll ditch the car somewhere, and take the first plane we can get out of Dubrovnik."

As they drove off at top speed, Klaus said angrily, almost resentfully, "It was absolute suicide to get out of the car while all that stuff was falling. The boy was crazy."

"What did you say?" Heinrich asked in astonishment as they drove rapidly on.

Stephen reached the top of the pass. All around him was scanty grass, on which a few cows grazed for their summer pasture. Stephen knew that, in actual fact, he was not especially high, about eight thousand feet, but none the less he had a feeling that he was on the very roof of the world.

He got out of the car for a moment to stretch his legs, which were aching, and the cool wind tossed his hair over his face. Behind him he saw bare limestone, cleft by the deep chasm of the Kurnovo gorge. Ahead, the road twisted down in an unending series of hairpin bends, but he saw that the land was more fertile, and fell, in the far distance, to a vivid green valley.

He told himself he had no time to waste, and climbed into the car again.

A short while before, even the previous day, the drive around all the hairpin bends would have terrified Stephen, but now he found that he could even allow for the repeated slight skids on the loose gravel. He went down, down, and still farther down. Once or twice, he saw men working in the fields, gathering the last of the hay with a strange implement that was rake and scythe combined. He saw a woman winnowing corn on a circular threshing floor, and behind her was a wooden shack. It was hard to tell if it was meant for animals or was her own dwelling. He decided that it was no use to stop and try to speak to any of them.

He wondered if, with the delay for the blowout, he had managed to beat the Fiat. Then, for the first time, he also wondered if he had gambled right. What if the Fiat had headed inland toward the E5 road?

At last, he came within sight of where his own road, still a dirt track, hit the main road to the coast. He saw the change of surface where the main road was tarred. Then he saw a white car coming from the direction of Starigrad. It was a very long way below him, and he was too late.

It passed by the junction of the two roads and swept on. It was almost out of sight before something registered in Stephen's mind. The car, to judge by its shape, had not been a Fiat at all. Roger could have told him that it was a Mercedes. He drove on.

He was several hairpin bends above the road junction when he first became aware of a wire fence, like a gigantic tennis-court fence, that stretched over the landscape for a distance of several miles. He was so busy staring at it that he nearly misjudged one of the bends.

It also distracted him from watching the other road, so that when he saw the Fiat it was almost straight beneath him with several bends in between them. Given that it was the more powerful car, and had, presumably, a much more experienced driver, would he ever manage to overtake it? It drove on, and Stephen, catching a quick glimpse into the car, had a confused impression that the back seat was empty.

Then the car pulled onto the grass shoulder and stopped.

Klaus wanted to stop for the simple reason that he, like Stephen, had found the drive very tiring. He said to Heinrich, "I'll hand the car over to you."

They both got out of the car and started to loosen the last remains of the broken windshield. When they had finished, they looked around.

Except for the incongruous note of the wire fence in the distance, it was a very peaceful, pastoral scene that must have changed little over the past centuries. There was no one in sight except for a young man in gray, who was leaning over the parapet of a bridge a short way ahead. Then a cart, pulled by two huge, patient-looking oxen, came into sight. It was driven by a handsome young woman in a dress with a long, many-layered skirt and with coins plaited into her hair. The young man in gray shouted a greeting to her.

"I must get this," muttered Heinrich, and seizing the camera, he went to the edge of the road to take a sideways view of the cart. He hastily checked the focus so that the woman and oxen would appear clearly and the intrusive fence not show at all. He clicked, the girl gave a sidelong smile, and then she drove on.

Stephen had now reached the level where the two roads met. From what he could see of the parked Fiat, there was no sign of Joey. Had Joey escaped, or had the men taken some steps to dispose of him?

He could not be sure if the men would recognize him and the car. When he reached the place where the two roads joined, he turned and drove a few yards along the road toward Starigrad. He was now facing the wrong way for following the Fiat, but the right way for escaping, if only he could find Joey. Trying to look like a casual sightseer, he strolled toward the Fiat.

Suddenly, he heard a loud shout. The young man who had been lounging on the parapet of the bridge woke up with a jolt. He started to hurry toward the Fiat, and Stephen saw with amazement that he carried a gun.

Heinrich, lowering his camera, heard the shout at the same moment. He was aware of somebody shouting, but felt that his best hope was to act the innocent tourist. He lifted his camera once more and photographed the man who was approaching him. Next moment, he felt the camera snatched out of his hands.

The strap of the camera was slung around his neck, and it caught on him painfully. He protested, and then felt the camera ripped away. He said angrily in German, "You can't do that."

The man snapped, *"Photographie verboten."* He flicked open the camera and made as if to take out the film.

Suddenly something happened to Heinrich, as if he had heard a note too high for human endurance. He had come on the trip as a frankly commercial proposition, because he knew that he could earn very much more working for Klaus than he could ever hope to make by selling his own paintings. But, just as Stephen had been, and with a better informed eye, he had been entranced by the paintings he had seen in Yugoslavia. So far as he was concerned, the camera contained not a reel of film, but his attempt to interpret a vision.

He reached hurriedly to close the camera before the film was ruined. The young man had his head bent to see what he was doing, and Heinrich hit him on the jaw by mistake.

The young man gave a shout of fury. Next moment, he had whipped out a rifle and pointed it at Heinrich's chest. Klaus yelled, "You imbecile! Don't you see it's the Army?"

At the sound, another man in gray approached from the far side of the bridge, hastily putting a cigarette out as he came. He shouted something that sounded like "Halt!" and pointed his rifle at Klaus.

Stephen was now only a few yards away. He stopped still, with his arms by his side. Then he wondered if it would be too melodramatic to put his hands up. The soldiers started to jabber furiously in what sounded like Serbian with an occasional word of German. From time to time they jerked their heads toward the wire fence.

Suddenly Stephen realized what must have happened. Once again, he tried to visualize the map in his mind, and he knew that they were very close to the Albanian border. The wire fence must be the actual border line.

He knew nothing about Albania except that it was allied to Communist China and had no links with any other nation in Europe. One of the boys at school had warned

95

him that relations between it and Yugoslavia were strained. It seemed likely that photography was forbidden in the zone between the two countries.

Stephen remembered reports he had read in the newspapers of British tourists arrested in Yugoslavia for photographing airports and other installations. If he remembered rightly, they had been sentenced to long terms of imprisonment.

To judge by the way the soldiers were talking, the fact that the two men spoke German made the whole matter worse. It sounded as if they were having some difficulty in explaining the difference between Swiss and German. The soldiers were little older than Stephen himself, so it might have seemed odd that they should still be upset by a war that had happened before they were born, but having heard Granddad talk of King Stephen, six hundred years dead, as a brother-in-arms, Stephen felt that he could believe anything of the Yugoslavs.

He stood stock still, for fear of alarming the soldiers, and stared hard into the car. There was no sign of Joey inside. Or could he be hidden down on the floor behind the front seats?

Stephen went forward, an inch or two at a time. It was almost like a game that small children play, when they try to sneak up behind a child who has his back turned. Except, Stephen thought grimly, that in that game you don't have guns.

He came up to a point where by turning his head a little, he could look into the car. Without any doubt, it was empty.

One of the soldiers said something that seemed to be the equivalent of "You'd better come along with me." He pushed the two men toward their car. It was obvious that he was telling them to drive off somewhere. For the first time, he became fully aware of Stephen, and gave him a curt nod of dismissal.

For one moment, Stephen hesitated. He wondered if he should try to explain to the soldiers about the picture and Joey. If he had been sure that he could communicate with them, he would have done so.

As it was, he felt helpless. He had visions of spending hours in a barracks or police station, perhaps even of getting arrested himself. It might be better to drive back toward Starigrad, and see if he could find any trace of what had happened to Joey.

So, still wishing that he could do something more effective, he gave a slight nod to the soldiers, and turned back toward his car.

11

There was no time to stop and think.

Joey had already maneuvered toward the car door, keeping one hand to open the door and the other to pull out the icon. At the instant when the glass of the windshield started to crack all over, Joey's fingers were already on the handle. By the time the car jerked to a halt, Joey had the door open a little and one leg dangling out. It was now or never.

The action of getting out of the car before it had quite stopped moving, while at the same time supporting the weight of the icon, nearly sent Joey sprawling onto the road. Then, without any time for recovery, came the question of which way to run.

Almost at once it became clear that there was no choice. Ahead was the car. On one side was steep rock, and on the other a drop. The only possible thing was to run back into the cloud of dust that marked the point of the explosion.

In one way, Joey knew, it was a sensible thing to do.

There was so much thick, choking, white dust that it was almost impossible to see ahead. Presumably, it would also serve to conceal anyone who was running away. But mixed up with the dust were sharp fragments of rock that were still raining down. Joey had no protection against them, for both hands were clutching the heavy icon. Could the icon itself serve as a shield? Before Joey had time to try this, another shower of rock came down. A lump struck Joey on the head, on the bright copper hair that was now white with dust.

Joey staggered on. The upward ground on one side of the road became less steep and seemed to offer a way of escape. Joey started to clamber up, hindered by the icon.

Although it was now late afternoon, the sun was still high in the sky, and the stone all around was giving out the stored-up heat of the day. The whiteness of the stone produced a dazzling glare. In the places where there was any vegetation, there was a strange, shimmering effect, as if the air were in constant motion with waves of color. It was, in fact, caused by countless butterflies, small blues and painted ladies, that were fluttering ceaselessly a few inches above the ground. Joey was finding it hard to focus.

Once, Joey stopped, put down the icon, and raised a hand to hair that was covered with dust. There was no sign of blood. Why, then, should there be so much pain? Joey knew it was necessary to pick up the icon again, to carry it out of sight of the pursuers, but as to who the pursuers were, recollection was faded and blurred. Joey's only consciousness was of very near and immediate things—the warm, sunbaked earth and the heavy scent of the vegetation. A few cicadas shrilled on an endless, high-pitched note that vibrated painfully through Joey's head, making thought harder than ever.

From time to time images flashed into Joey's mind, images of faces known in the past and now nearly forgotten. There was the face of the art expert, Petar Metkovic, which was, at the same time, welcoming and a threat, then a sudden vision of two English boys. Who were they? They had some connection with what was happening now, but how could that be? There was something, thought Joey. . . . They had made some silly mistake, and I let them go on believing it. . . . They called me Joey . . . *Joey?*

Joey stared around at the barren land and up at the heavens, as if the racing clouds could provide some answer, and then spoke aloud in terror.

"I don't know what my name really is."

So Joey, who knew no other name, wandered, conscious of blinding headache, but not of other pain like that from short, whippy plants the drew blood from the ankles. Once Joey was even unaware of a poisonous snake only a few inches away. Any doctor would have diagnosed mild concussion and loss of memory from the blow on the head, but Joey did not realize this and was only surprised to be shivering in the heat.

It was impossible to tell what was real and what was hallucination. Several times Joey stumbled, having lost the power to judge distances and tell the position of things in space.

Yet, all the time, some impulse drove Joey, weighed down by the icon, on and on upward, a tiny dot against the vast expanse of the landscape.

In a brief moment of clear-headedness, Joey gazed around and on one side looked down at a forest. The trees, which were oaks and beeches, were of astonishing height, so that the clearings looked like deep pools in rock, full of impenetrable shadow. Here and there stood a tree that had been blasted by lightning, and stripped bare of all bark. The twisted white shapes, with their jagged, pointed limbs, stood out in sharp contrast to the lush, dark green of the other trees. It was too extreme, too wildly romantic, to offer any comfort to Joey's tormented mind; it only echoed the confusion within.

Nothing was left but that strange impulse to keep climbing upward.

Gradually, the pictures that had been crowding Joey's mind faded, and now came a period of near blankness. At last, Joey stopped from sheer exhaustion, rested the weight of the icon upon a rock, and stared at it unseeingly. Time, of which Joey was quite unaware, went past. Then the gravity of the Virgin's face, her air of knowing all the pain in the world, started to penetrate the turmoil in Joey's brain, and a coherent thought came out.

I am sure that this painting is very old. It reminds me of the icons I saw when Petar took me to Ohrid, before we quarreled. He could tell me just what it is. But Petar would think of it as a painting and nothing more. He forgets that once it stood in a church where it had a value beyond what its value is as a work of art. That's one reason why I must save it.

So Joey picked up the icon again, and went on climbing. The movement was monotonous and brought a thundering rush of blood to the ears, which gradually changed to a phantom sound of chanting.

"Especially our most holy, most pure, most blessed and glorious Lady, Mary, ever Virgin and Mother of God.

"More honorable than the cherubim, and glorious incomparably more than the seraphim . . . thee do we magnify."

The voices were those of the monks of the Bogorodica

Monastery, the Monastery of the Mother of God, chanting the Orthodox Liturgy.

But I don't believe it myself, thought Joey.

Or do I?

Joey had lost all sense of time, and, at moments, all sense of surroundings. Everything seemed limitless, and without definition. There was only one fixed point in the universe, and that was the icon. By some freak functioning of the brain, Joey was able to recognize what it was, while everything else, even an awareness of personal identity, had become buried.

In the Orthodox church an icon is thought of as a link between the visible and the invisible world. The abbot explained this to me. Many Yugoslavs, especially the older ones, would believe that this icon could work a miracle and protect me. Do I believe it myself? Am I that sort of person? I can't remember.

On and on up, until Joey came to the highest point of the mountains that separated the new road from the Kurnovo gorge.

It was now evening, and the keen wind had died down, so that the sky was completely still. The air was a very delicate, bluish pink, and so were the bare limestone mountains that stretched all around. Looking into the distance, it was impossible to tell what was mountain and what was sky, for it was all only an expression of light. The one solid thing in sight was the jagged silhouette of a solitary thorn bush; everything else was light, without substance, without definition.

The effect on someone in Joey's strange mental state was alarming. It was as if this were no longer a part of the normal world, as if all laws of time and space could be disregarded. Joey's stumbling pace turned into a labored run. Somewhere, in that point where the earth and the sky became one, there must be an answer, but to what, Joey could not tell.

The ground was sloping uphill toward the peak of a little ridge. Joey's eyes and brain registered nothing, but something, perhaps the nerve endings in the feet and the muscles in the calf of the leg, were conscious of this. Something, whatever it was, made Joey stop before the brow of the ridge, and from there look over.

In contrast to the glowing light all around, there was nothing but darkness below. At first the darkness was only a withdrawal of light, but farther down it became solid, like a thing you could touch and feel.

Out of the darkness came noise, faint but inexorable and unceasing, as of water that rushed and battered its way through a narrow defile. A current of very cold air rose up, and for a moment the coldness cleared Joey's brain.

This, Joey knew, was the very edge of a chasm. Just in front was a sheer drop of three thousand feet into the Kurnovo gorge.

12

Stephen had only driven a little way before an alarming thought struck him. What if Joey had been made unconscious and bundled into the trunk of the car?

He pulled to the side of the road, and wondered what he should do. If he went back, would the soldiers and the two Swiss still be there? Almost certainly, he decided, they would have driven off by now. Would the soldiers have searched the trunk before leaving? How long could anyone breathe shut up like that?

In the end he made up his mind to drive back to Starigrad and seek further help. There was still a chance that Joey might have escaped. As he drove around each bend, Stephen half expected to see Joey sitting by the side of the road, his jauntiness only a little dimmed, and full of abuse at Stephen for not having come before.

From time to time, he passed someone on the road—a herdsman bringing his sheep and goats down from the mountain, an old woman with a bundle of wool in one hand and a spindle in the other, spinning away as she walked. He tried to think of the phrases he had carefully learned, to see if he could communicate with them, but all he could think of was, "How much . . . ?" and "What is the way to . . . ?" He had a phrase book and dictionary at the farm, but they would not tell him how to say, "Have you seen a boy who carries an icon?"

The tarred surface made very easy driving compared to the drive up the Kurnovo gorge. A few cars passed him, and once he met a bus going in the other direction and had to back up on a bend.

Then he came to the point where the road was still unsurfaced. The men had given up work for the evening, but there were obvious signs of recent activity. Stephen got out of the car and looked around. If Joey had contrived to escape, this would have been an obvious place, for his captors would have had to go slowly, perhaps to stop. Could there possibly be a clue? Stephen entertained wild hopes of finding a handkerchief, neatly named, fluttering from some bush. Then he wondered if there might be footprints among the dust. He tried to visualize what Joey wore on his feet, and had a vague picture of thonged sandals. All he could make out for certain was the imprint of a workman's heavy boots.

Joey's feet were quite small, weren't they? Small, and unlike so many feet, well-shaped. They were covered with dust and scratches, but the nails were carefully cut, and his ankles were slender.

"Am I crazy to start thinking about another boy's feet?" Stephen asked himself, almost resentfully. With one last look around, he got back into the car, and drove as fast as he could toward Starigrad.

It was on the outskirts of the town that he ran into trouble. It was starting to get dark. There were no street

105

lights, but lights were switched on under the trees in front gardens, showing small groups of men sitting drinking, or women preparing the evening meal with the help of an outside tap. Trees on either side of the road caused still deeper shadows, so Stephen was not aware of trouble until he heard a frantic flapping and squawking just in front of the car.

Someone was keeping a cock in his garden, and Stephen had nearly run over it.

The cock flapped his way up onto a gatepost and began to express his views on people who attacked innocent birds. A woman seemed to be telling the cock that it was exaggerating. Stephen, who had stopped, called out, "Sorry," which was one of the words he had learned. Then a man who had been drinking in one of the gardens got up, glancing at his watch and buckling his belt. A light shone down on him. It was a policeman going on duty.

He came up to Stephen and Stephen smiled. The cock was obviously in the best of health, if not indeed stimulated by the encounter. There was nothing to worry about. The policeman said something, and Stephen smiled again.

Then he suddenly realized. He was being accused of driving without a rear light.

Even so, Stephen could not feel that it was anything very serious. He showed his driving license and insurance certificate, and tried meanwhile to explain that it was far more important for the police to find out what had happened to Joey than to bother about his lights.

The policeman spoke neither English, French, nor German, and had no wish to try. So far, his attitude might have been defined as being negatively obstructive.

Stephen tried his few words of Serbian. He managed

to put together, "Mrs. MacLeod's young son needs help."
The man shook his head, and said obstinately, "Mrs.
MacLeod has no son."

Stephen, who had been convinced he had got the words
right, sighed. Then, unfortunately for himself, he had an
inspiration.

Of the languages that he learned in school, the one
most closely related to the various languages spoken in
Yugoslavia was Russian. Suppose he tried talking in Russian? He began, very slowly and clearly.

The policeman knew enough Russian to recognize the
language, for he had been at school just after the war,
when Russia was Yugoslavia's chief foreign friend. He
had been a young man when the break with Russia had
come, along with all the disillusionment that had followed. He knew that at that very moment, men were
awaiting trial on a charge of trying to restore Russian
influence and overthrow the regime.

Hope rose up in him. He had had an undistinguished
career. Was this a possible moment of glory? This could
be no ordinary English boy, who spoke French and German fluently and had just given away that he spoke
Russian as well. It would not be going against his country's
traditions to arrest first, and ask questions afterward.

In the end, Klaus and Heinrich seemed to have the
better of it. Titograd barracks, where they were held on
a charge of assaulting a soldier in the execution of his
duty, was an up-to-date prestige building. Starigrad jail
was not, and its sanitation was medieval in the worst sense
of the word.

It was there that Stephen was taken, on the suspicion
of being a Russian spy.

13

As to what happened from then on, Joey was not quite certain.

There was a long moment of staring down into the darkness, listening to the thunder of the stream so far below. There was no terror, only an awful fascination, as if it would be such an easy solution to let oneself slide down there, and be overwhelmed.

Then came a shivering that heralded the normal human reaction of fear.

Somehow Joey clambered back from the edge of the precipice, but now the moments of lost consciousness were coming closer together and were more intense. There was an overpowering wish to lie down and sleep, to rest, to stop trying to remember. Joey's sight was beginning to fail.

In fact, it was the light itself that was fading. The blues, the pinks, and the faint trace of gold all changed into pearly gray, and then lost all luster and went dull. The air thickened, and space contracted.

An almost animal instinct led Joey to the shelter of an overhanging rock. There was a little opening there, much less than a cave, into which it was possible to wedge one's body. A primitive desire for protection led Joey to wriggle in there. The world outside seemed threatening and immense, so Joey pulled the icon across the opening, just leaving a little space for the air to come in. Inside it was very dark. The effort of getting in had made Joey's head spin worse than ever, but now it was possible to lie down, to let go completely. Within seconds, Joey was in a state halfway between loss of consciousness and natural sleep.

Was the next part an illusion?

Was it the result of a blow on the head, of climbing too fast, of the sun's heat reflected off the bare rock, and of increasing thirst? Was it the final stage in a flight from reality?

Or did it really happen?

Joey, half waking, thought to feel the ground vibrate as something approached the shelter. Then there was a snuffling noise as some creature sniffed around. Time dragged on, with the sound of breathing, and soft, padding footsteps.

Joey went cold with terror. There were bears in this wild country. Wolves, too, lived up in the mountains, only coming down to the villages in the harsh depths of winter. Whatever this creature might be, was this its lair? Did that mean it was coming in?

The only protection was one piece of wood, the icon. A single blow from the animal's paw could bring it crashing down.

There was a moment of absolute silence. Had the animal gone away? The breathing sounded louder, and then came a grunt. Joey lay there, muscles locked rigid with fear.

The grunt turned into a rasping noise. Joey could not imagine what it might be. It was like a sound often made by a cat, on a vastly magnified scale. It was the noise of licking.

The creature was drawing its tongue backward and forward across the gold surface to see what it was.

It took an immense effort of will for Joey to open one eye and glance out. The moon must have risen, for there was a sharp crack of light beside the edge of the icon.

Joey lay there and waited.

Suddenly, the light was blotted out as the creature moved.

Fear and exhaustion were too much. Joey lost consciousness.

A few hours later, Joey awoke. The icon, which had been blocking the mouth of the little shelter, had fallen down and lay painted side upward. It was too dark to see the subject, but the gold background shimmered a bit in the moonlight.

Joey, stiff, hungry, tired, but now completely clear-headed, managed to scramble out.

The moonlight was so bright that it had an almost fierce quality, as though it could burn with cold. It illuminated every crevice of the stone upland, and every spike of the scant vegetation that grew there.

"What in heaven's name am I doing here?" said Joey aloud. "Of all the stupid places to be!"

There was no clue as to what had happened, except for a focal point of pain on one side of Joey's head.

"I suppose I may have been hit on the head, and am

suffering from partial amnesia, or whatever they call it."
Joey touched the spot carefully and then winced. "But
I do know that I'm cold, and I'm stiff and I'm tired.
I'm hungry and thirsty and everything else, *and* I want
to get out of here."

So saying, Joey started to go downhill, still talking aloud
because the sound of a human voice, even one's own,
was reassuring.

"I was in a place. . . . Was I dreaming? I was looking
down . . . into something . . . half terrified I would fall,
and half wanting to let myself go. But even that wasn't
the worst. There was an animal—a bear or a wolf—and
it might have attacked me, but I was saved by a miracle-
working icon from the Monastery of the Mother of God.

"What absolute nonsense!" said Joey.

Then memory began to come flooding back. There
might or might not have been a wild animal, but somewhere there was an icon, somewhere on this moon-
flooded mountainside. Joey went hurrying upward.

At first it seemed an impossible task to find anything
in that light, so bright and yet so deceiving. Then, on
flat ground beside a large rock, Joey saw it.

The air was very still in the shelter of the rock, and
it seemed as if a faint animal scent hung there.

Did I dream it? thought Joey. Or did an animal really
come and smell that I was there? I thought I heard it
breathing. But the icon was blocking the entrance. Did
it save me?

Joey bent down to pick up the icon, and without even
meaning to speak, said words never consciously learned,
but heard from the monks at the monastery.

"Mother of God, most holy Lady, light of my darkened
soul, my hope, my shelter, and my refuge."

14

As time went on, however, it became clear that Klaus and Heinrich were not doing too well. Normally someone who is arrested in a foreign country asks to see his own consul. But the last thing on earth Klaus wanted was the Swiss consul. What if it was ever discovered that a highly respected art dealer from Zürich was traveling on a false passport?

In that one impulsive moment of grabbing the icon he might have destroyed a position built up by years of careful planning. In the meantime all he could do, and he glared at Heinrich to do the same, was to apologize, even grovel. Whatever happened, they must get away from here before anybody connected them with the icon and that unspeakable redheaded boy.

Klaus tried to review what he knew of Yugoslavia. It had a reputation for harsh penalties on foreigners breaking its laws. But it was a federation of states, more than a single country, with different languages, even different alphabets. They had taken the picture in Serbia, and Heinrich had hit the soldier in Montenegro. It was a fine thing, Klaus thought bitterly, that their hopes should rest upon bureaucratic muddle.

Stephen's arrival at what he promptly christened "the old jailhouse" at Starigrad, was the event of the year there. Everyone thought he was far too interesting to put away in a cell, so he was invited to join in the meal which some of the men on duty had had sent in from a nearby café. It was, Stephen decided, a mush-up of goat's meat and eggplants, which in his hungry state tasted delicious. With it, he drank a good deal more red wine than he was accustomed to. He began to enjoy himself, and a number of people came in to see him. All of them had a drink. With the forces of law and order so occupied, it was a good night for crime in Starigrad.

Then it occurred to the police to make a thorough search of the car. Luckily, Roger and Stephen had unpacked most of their belongings and left them in their tent at the farm. What remained proved fascinating to all concerned. Roger's bright-red underpants, which were found stuck under one of the seats, were particularly admired.

In between all this, Stephen tried to find out how much longer he would be kept there. He asked to see Joey's mother, or the abbot of the Bogorodica Monastery. Everyone thought that for a Russian spy to ask for the abbot was very extraordinary, and must therefore be very sinister. They looked at Stephen with ever-mounting respect. Then one of the policemen who spoke a little English pointed out that on the red pants was written the mysterious legend "St. Michael." By now, Stephen suspected, they had decided he was part of a plot to overthrow Yugoslavia hatched up between Russia and the Pope.

This led to a search for more hidden messages. They found the stickers that Roger's and Stephen's friends had given them, and which Stephen had stuck onto the inside of the car. They were all carefully peeled off and taken into the police station.

Some passed without comment. One, of a girl in a bikini, was subjected to a great deal of scrutiny, but it seemed to be of an unpolitical nature. One, which simply said *Leeds United,* was met with applause. Then came the sinister one. It commanded briefly,

REMEMBER YOU'RE A WOMBLE

The policeman who spoke a little English said that "womble" was not a real English word, and produced a dictionary to prove it. Everybody became very excited. Someone went home on a bicycle and came back with what seemed to be the Yugoslav version of *Every Schoolboy's Book on How to Crack Codes.*

They all sat down with paper and pen. Stephen, bemused with red wine and excitement, joined them.

At some stage there was a telephone call to say that a man had tried to cut his wife's throat. There was a general feeling that this was a purely domestic affair, and a very junior policeman was sent off to deal with it.

Not long afterward, Granddad stormed in to ask for news of a young member of his family, who, he alleged, had been kidnapped. One of the policemen shut the door on the happy band of decoders, and went to try to calm him down. He pointed out that the person concerned was a British subject by birth and held a British passport, so that it was not entirely his responsibility.

Granddad expressed his views on the uselessness of the police with a great deal of vigor.

The policeman then said, rather rashly, that to judge by gossip in Starigrad, the first place to look for the missing relation would be in the company of Dr. Petar Metkovic of the National Museum in Belgrade. At this point, Granddad was nearly arrested for striking a guardian of the law, but fortunately, the policeman ducked just in time.

In the end, Granddad swept out of the police station, muttering darkly, and the policeman went thankfully back to the far more interesting business of dealing with Starigrad's first-ever international spy.

In a tent in the plum orchard by the farmhouse, Roger lay trying to sleep. He could feel the muscles of his hands and his jaw and his thighs clenching and growing tense. He tried consciously to relax, but all he could do was to mutter, "If I had known before, would it have made any difference?"

Inside the farmhouse, Granddad was raging, and Mrs. MacLeod was attempting to calm him.

"The one you ought to be worrying about, Father, is the English boy who has disappeared as well. He struck me as rather a dreamer, not a practical sort at all. First thing in the morning, we will have to contact his father, and let him know what has happened. But Joey will be all right, I think. Joey is very much like me."

She stared at the photograph of the four youths dressed as Partisans. There was still a conspicuous likeness between the youngest fighter with a belt full of hand grenades and the middle-aged woman.

115

She said, "Two of them are dead, and one is a cripple. But I fought along with them all the way, and I was the one who survived."

In the Monastery of the Mother of God, a handful of monks were singing the night prayer. A few thin candles flickered in the church, and a faint haze of moonlight came in through the tiny windows set very high in the walls.

Elsewhere in the monastery, a light was still burning up in the dusty, untidy library, where manuscripts were piled in heaps and someone had hung bunches of herbs to dry from the rafters. Dr. Petar Metkovic, expert on Serbo-Byzantine art, was crouched over a manuscript written in Old Slavonic. Open on the table beside him was another book, which looked typically nineteenth-century, being calf-bound with marbled edges and endpapers. It was in English and bore the title, *Travels in the Slavonic Provinces of Turkey-in-Europe.* It had been written over a hundred years earlier by two intrepid Victorian ladies who had traveled the area with a view to improving the education of girls there. Being of an inquiring nature, they had investigated everything they could come across, including the caves in the Kurnovo gorge.

At last, Petar gathered the papers together and stood up. Down below him, the sound of chattering had ceased. There was the creak of a hinge as a heavy door was opened, then the faint patter of sandaled feet on the cobblestones. He hurried downstairs and stood waiting under the eaves as the monks crossed the moonlit court-yard.

Standing there, as if tensed for action, he looked quite remarkably unlike an expert on Serbo-Byzantine art. He

116

was a man in his late twenties, six and a half feet tall, with flowing black hair and beard. He came from Montenegro—the Black Mountain—which breeds such magnificent fighting men that they had for century after century kept free of the Turkish invaders.

Petar was a very twentieth-century man, an atheist and a member of the Yugoslav Communist party, but it was with no sense of betraying his principles that he went up to the last figure to cross the courtyard, and quietly said, "My lord."

The abbot stopped, and looked up at the younger man. The other monks all went into their dormitories.

"You could well be right," said Petar. "If only I had known about those caves before. All that the Chronicle says is that it was carefully hidden when the Turks came, along with much of the church plate and the Chronicle itself. When you told me that the Chronicle had been kept in the rafters, and the plate down the well, I assumed that this treasure too must be somewhere inside the monastery walls. It seemed much the safest place to hide it.

"But if hermits had lived in those caves for years, and they were in effect little chapels, then one of them might have been used as a hiding place. Yet it seems odd that the Turks never looked at all, when those two Victorian ladies had only to see the caves to start scrambling up. And the English boy now is the same."

"Maybe that is the difference between the Turks and the English," the abbot suggested. "Does the Chronicle say what it looked like at all?"

"It says nothing. At least, nothing that I as an art historian find to the point. The only description it gives is that 'all men shall recognize it by the miracles that it works.' "

The moonlight shone on the whites of his eyes, and

made deep shadows under his cheek bones. He looked tormented.

"Then if that is what they have really found, we shall be able to see if the statement is true," said the abbot impassively. "Perhaps it will save Joey."

"Do you honestly believe such things? All I know is that if those men have hurt Joey I feel I could tear them apart with my own bare hands."

"Not that, I beg you," the abbot said. He stretched out his own hands, and the heavy antique ring that he wore flashed in the moonlight. "Not that," and his lips tightened, as if in unhappy remembrance.

Stephen slept uneasily on a concrete slab in a police cell, and in his sleep he weaved around hairpin bends with precipices beside him. The tumult of a mountain river roared in his ears, and meaningless words beat at his brain.

"Womble, wobble, gobble, gabble."

A tire had just burst, and he hung there, looking down into the abyss.

The colonel at Titograd barracks slammed the airline timetable down on his desk. It was four o'clock in the morning.

He said, "You will be driven to Dubrovnik airport, and from there you will be put on the first plane to Switzerland. With luck, you will catch a flight to Geneva this morning. In any case, my men will remain with you until you board the plane. Your passports will be given to the captain and he will return them to you when you reach Switzerland. That car of yours will be put on the ferry to Italy, and what becomes of it then will be up to you. I have taken money to cover all your expenses. Can you tell me of any reason why you should not be deported?"

Heinrich seemed about to speak, but Klaus silenced him with a glance. To get out of Yugoslavia without his identity being discovered exceeded his wildest hopes. He wondered what would happen if there were no seats on the plane, but decided the colonel would probably order some innocent passenger or two off the plane.

He said in a very noncommittal voice, "I understand, Colonel," and gazed at the large pile of currency, mainly Swiss francs and dollars, which the colonel had confiscated from his briefcase. He did a quick calculation as to what this disastrous trip had cost him, and for one wild moment he toyed with the idea of querying the colonel's arithmetic, or even of asking for a receipt to set the whole thing down as a loss against income tax.

Then, at a curt nod from the colonel, he and Heinrich went outside, to where an army driver was waiting for them.

As Klaus climbed into the car, he wondered how long the journey to Dubrovnik would take, and when the next plane would leave. At present, he had no idea what he would do when they landed, perhaps at an airport many miles from home, but much the most important thing was to get out of Yugoslavia as quickly as possible. Everything depended on what he termed "the redheaded brat." What if he had been killed by the blasting and his body had been found? Would the other boys have been able to tell the police enough to link his disappearance with Heinrich and Klaus? Worse still, what if the brat had survived, and had managed to tell the whole story?

15

The first news reached the farmhouse next morning, when they were just finishing breakfast. The twins in their baggy Turkish trousers came fluttering in, obviously excited, but even so sparing a moment to bat their eyelids at Roger. They spoke to Mrs. MacLeod.

"What's happened?" demanded Roger. "Is it Stephen or Joey?"

"It's Stephen's car. A friend of theirs lives in a house that overlooks the back of Starigrad police station. There is a small car with a Great Britain license plate registration parked in the police-station yard. We'll go down to Starigrad right away. Perhaps we'll go to the twins' friend first, and look out of their window. Do you know the number of the car, Roger?"

Roger nodded.

It was indeed Stephen's car, but they could not imagine what it was doing there. They went into the police station, and, with a confidence that they did not feel, asked for news of Stephen himself. The police, in the end, admitted that he was there, but said he was being held on a charge so important that a senior official was even then on the way to see him. Nobody might talk to him in the meantime.

Mrs. MacLeod launched into a flood of Serbian, in which Roger kept on hearing the name "Joey," but it availed nothing.

They sat down and waited.

And waited.

At long last, the senior policeman arrived, accompanied by a younger man laden with papers. He swept in to see Stephen, looking arrogant and composed, and swept out a few minutes later looking decidedly angry. He snapped out something that obviously meant that his time had been wasted. Then he turned on Mrs. MacLeod, who, in turn, looked at Roger.

"He says it is all really Stephen's fault that anyone ever imagined that he was a spy. I am not at all sure what it is all about, but it does seem that Stephen behaved very oddly last night. But he wants to know all about Joey as well."

So once again, Roger tried to explain how the two men had taken Joey. Luckily Stephen was then released. He told how he had seen the men arrested on the Albanian border, but that there had been no sign of Joey at all.

Mrs. MacLeod, struggling to keep down her own anxiety, had to interpret. She kept passing on questions to them.

"Are you sure it was the army who arrested the men? What sort of uniforms were they wearing?"

"Which way did they take them?"

"Yes, it must have been toward Titograd if they took that road."

"Did you see the men well enough to describe them?"

There was another long pause, while someone put through a telephone call to army headquarters at Titograd. At one point he gave a nod to confirm that this was, in fact, the right place. They waited again, then a conversation began of which the boys could make out nothing at all.

They both fidgeted restlessly, while Mrs. MacLeod stood very still, with her hands clasped tightly together. When at last there was news they could see that it distressed her.

"The two men have already been put on a flight to Geneva. The army will ring Dubrovnik airport to see if they can get a radio message to the pilot. He will be told to detain them on board, and to contact the Swiss police when they arrive."

"So what happens now?" said Roger.

"All we can do is to wait. You two had better go back to the farm, just in case, by a miracle, Joey turns up there. I will wait here for news. The police say you can take your car provided that you only use it during daytime until the light has been mended. They say if they catch you driving at night again, they will put you back into the cell, and this time really keep you there."

"No, thank you very much," said Stephen, who was not in the least certain if this was a joke or a threat. He shook hands with his erstwhile jailers, and they parted on friendly terms, but he sighed with relief to be back in the sunshine again.

As they drove up the valley, Roger said, "They didn't mistreat you, did they? Knock you around, or anything like that? You're looking pretty shaken."

"They only arrested me without any charge, and kept me locked up on a crazy suspicion. On what you might call a personal level, they were extremely friendly."

Nothing on earth would have made Stephen admit the police had been so hospitable that he was suffering from a hangover.

They walked slowly into the farmhouse, both hesitating on the threshold, as if reluctant to enter it when Joey was not there.

Everything was the same as it had been when they first saw the room less than two long days before, except that an icon now stood in the niche beside Marshal Tito's portrait. At once it was obvious that the niche had been made for an icon, and that the man who had built the house had meant it to be the focal point of the room.

A little oil lamp was hung underneath the icon, and a girl was bending to light it. Her gestures were slow, deliberate, almost ceremonial. She was a figure from countless Byzantine paintings, in a black shirt heavily encrusted with gold, and a deep-plum-colored skirt that fell in folds to the floor. Around her neck was string after string of gold beads, and her hands were so covered with rings that her fingers were stiff.

She had not heard them enter the room, for her entire attention was fixed on the icon. Only when the lamp was lighted did she turn around and see them. She stood and looked at them, motionless, hardly even blinking. She had made up her eyes with green-gold eyeshadow, which made them look enormous, and added to her stylized, artificial appearance, but the eyes themselves were human and very tired.

Roger thought, "She's not my sort of girl at all. But I think when you get used to her, she'd make most other girls seem boring."

He had suspected the truth about her from the moment when he had suddenly seen her gazing up at the icon which he was lowering from the cave. The shock of the ledge crumbling under his feet, the kidnapping, and Stephen's disappearance had made him mistrust the evidence of his own eyes, and so he had said nothing to Stephen.

Stephen was totally unprepared. Delight at seeing her safe and anger at the trick she had played on them mixed with another emotion which he identified as relief. The odd mixture of hostility and attraction that Joey had sometimes aroused in him was explained.

Joey?

He said doubtfully, "Is your name Josephine?"

"Or Joanna?" Roger suggested.

She shook her head.

"No, it can't be," said Stephen. "There is something I knew all along, which I had completely forgotten. In the Yugoslav languages, the letter *j* is pronounced as if it were a *y*. I remember telling one of the boys from school that, before we came. So a Yugoslav would have pronounced your name *Yoey*. Instead it was more like a *dz* sound. So what would your name really be?"

Still she did not speak.

"I know what it is at the back of my mind," Stephen went on. "It was in one of those books that I read. A name that several of the empresses of Byzantium had. Are you called Zoë?"

"Yes," said Zoë. She inclined her head a little, and behind her there were the faint ghosts of other Zoës, who had once inclined their heads to receive a crown.

"What made you pretend that you were a boy?" asked Roger.

"I wouldn't say I pretended at all. It was you who took it for granted. You told one another that I was a boy as soon as you saw me. I suppose it was partly the clothes. That jerkin is pretty stiff and shapeless. In fact, it is the

top half of my great-grandmother's costume, and the
reason I wasn't wearing the skirt is because I found it
too bulky and awkward for driving the cart. And my hair
is shorter than yours, of course, and I've often been told
that I walk like a boy. But if you'd asked me in so many
words, I'd have told you the truth right away."

"Only why did you do it at all?" Stephen insisted.

"For very personal reasons. A good many people I
know, and especially Petar, treat me primarily as a girl
and not simply as a person. He thinks of me only in
relation to himself, and not in my own right. So when
you assumed I was a boy, I thought that this meant that
you would treat me as *me*. It was Mother really who
gave me the idea. She joined the Partisans when she
was younger than I am now, and all the while they were
fighting together, they simply had to forget about her
being a girl."

"And did it work?" Stephen insisted.

"No, I can't say it did entirely. I wanted the sensation
of being treated as an equal. But you assumed that I
must be several years younger than you, and so you
adjusted your manner accordingly. If I told you to do
something, you thought I was being uppish, and if I
happened to know something, you thought I was a precocious brat."

For the first time, she smiled, but the boys looked at
one another a little guiltily.

"Then how old are you?" said Roger.

"I think I am a year older than you are. That is to
say, I have finished my first year at Belgrade University.
It makes one feel quite a lot older than someone who's
just left school. And you know what they say about girls
being older than boys for their age anyhow."

She walked restlessly to the window. In the daylight

it was possible to see her clothes properly for the first time. The shirt was simply embroidered cheesecloth, of the sort sold in boutiques and street markets all over Europe. The long skirt was no ritual vestment, but any girl's alternative to jeans. As for the mass of rings and necklaces, they probably came, Stephen thought, from the Yugoslav version of Woolworth's. His sister, the girls at school, and his girl friends all covered themselves with beads like that.

Then the sunlight flared on her copper hair and turned it into a halo of light like that around the head of the young archangel at the monastery, or into a golden crown on the head of an empress. It shone, too, on her face, which was no longer that of a girl, but of a grown woman, with the heavy smudges under the eyes and the look of near exhaustion. Once again Stephen was haunted by a resemblance. It was the face of the Empress Theodora, cast into mosaics fourteen hundred years earlier.

No wonder she says that she's old, he thought. She's as old as Byzantium.

It was left to Roger to ask, "How many people know that you're back? Have you told the police?"

"No. I got a lift back here from someone I met, and when I arrived there was nobody in but Granddad. I sent him to look for Mother. I suppose I shall have to make a statement and so on, but I felt I had to eat and get cleaned up before I could face doing anything. Do you know what became of those men? The only thing I was interested in was getting away from them."

They sat at the table to tell her all they knew. Meanwhile Zoë, with the first consciously feminine gesture that they had seen in her, painted her fingernails. Even this increased her exotic appearance, for the nail polish was

126

gold. She seemed very determined to make herself some-one as far removed as possible from the boylike figure that they had known.

"Now tell us what happened to you," said Stephen. "How did you escape from those men? I drove all the way down the road you had taken, and I couldn't decide what had happened. How did you ever get out of the car? And where did you go when you had?"

Zoë stretched out her hand and stared hard at her gold-painted nails, as if she found reassurance in the trivial actions of life.

"I hid," she said at last, in her voice that was very low-pitched for a girl.

"Where did you hide, though? You must have stayed out all night."

"Yes," said Zoë.

"What did you do?"

"How did you get away from them?"

"Zoë, are you quite sure that those men really didn't hurt you?"

There was a long silence.

"Nothing hurt me," said Zoë in an odd voice. She got up and stood staring at the icon.

"I suppose the police will take charge of the icon now," said Roger, trying to break the slight feeling of tension.

"They mustn't!" Zoë exclaimed.

"But you can't very well keep it here in your house. Nobody knows whose it is. They will have to put it in a museum," said Stephen.

"No," Zoë said flatly.

"Be realistic. You can't stop them."

Zoë stood motionless, staring all the time at the icon.

"It must not go to a museum," she said at last. "It

would be stuck up on a wall with a catalog number, and crowds of sightseers filing past it. It was never painted for that."

She stretched up and took the icon into her arms, which ached once again with its familiar weight.

"But you can't put it back in the cave!" Stephen objected.

"No, it doesn't belong in the cave either. I am going to take it to the abbot. He will know what to do with it. Only we must hurry, in case Granddad has told everyone that I am home, and the police come to see me and take it away."

16

By the time the message got through to Dubrovnik airport, the plane bearing Klaus and Heinrich was out of radio contact. There was then some argument between the police at Starigrad and the army authorities as to which of them should telephone the police in Geneva. The colonel who had seen Klaus and Heinrich outranked the senior policeman who had been called in to deal with Stephen. On the other hand, the policeman objected. Klaus and Heinrich were wanted for seizing Zoë Mac-Leod, which was a civil and not a military offense. It was finally agreed that the police might make a joint approach on behalf of them both.

After this matter of protocol had been settled, they had to wait some time until an international line was available. When at last it was, an electrical storm over the Alps made reception extremely bad. Then came the problem of what language to talk in. This was the French-speaking part of Switzerland, and the Yugoslavs could not speak French. The Swiss, however, spoke German, but with a Swiss-German accent, which was almost unintelligible to the Yugoslavs, whose own German was very indifferent. It was difficult to be confident that they had got the message across.

In fact, they had. The Geneva police promptly informed the airport police that two suspected kidnappers were due to arrive shortly on a flight from Dubrovnik. They sent a car to the airport themselves, which arrived at the exact moment when there was a major airport alert. A plane coming in from Milan had been badly struck by the storm and was about to land. Ambulances rushed to the airport and the runway was lined with fire engines, ready to drench the aircraft with foam.

Within sight of the airport, the lightning flickered and darted around the sharp peaks of Mont Blanc, the highest mountain in Europe.

Stephen, Roger, and Zoë climbed into the car, and Zoë sat in front clutching the icon. When they reached the monastery, she would not let them take it from her, but walked across the courtyard, her long skirt trailing behind her, with the icon held high in her gold-tipped hands as if she were carrying it in a procession. Two peacocks, the birds which the Byzantines used as the symbol of eternity, peered down at her from the roof of the church, and stretched their long, shimmering tails.

She went into the wide entrance porch of the church, which was painted with figures of emperors and archangels. A very tall man who was standing there spun around and exclaimed, "Zoë!" He stepped forward and would have put his arms around her, but she held the icon between them.

"Petar, this is Roger, and this is Stephen," she said, as if determined to keep the emotional temperature low.

"Dr. Petar Metkovic," she said, willing him to shake hands with the boys. Then, still ignoring the way he was looking at her, she went on, "Petar, we have found you another icon."

Petar ignored the icon, and said, "Zoë!" again.

Stephen's own feelings for Zoë were sufficiently aroused for him to understand something of what Petar was feeling. He thought, Petar assumes it's a game on her part, and that one day she will give in. Girls have never had any real alternative to getting married. But in our generation they have, especially someone like Zoë. I think she secretly sees herself as the first woman President of Yugoslavia.

Roger, whose own emotions were unaffected, thought along different lines. He really is rather overpowering. If I were her, I'd run.

In an effort to lower the tension, Zoë held out the icon toward Petar, but still she kept a tight hold of it. He looked at it for the first time, and exclaimed in his own language, "Holy Mother of God!"

Stephen, who understood the words, thought it was less a description of the picture than a cry from the heart.

"Do you know what it is?" asked Stephen.

"What do you expect me to say?" asked Petar, in careful, rather precise English that sounded a little incongruous from so powerful a man. "I am trained to be cautious, and not to jump to conclusions. This painting is very dirty, and I'm seeing it in a bad light. Officially, I will tell you that it looks very interesting, and should be examined carefully. Speaking just as myself, I would say it is thirteenth-century, very probably by the same artist as the icon of the Annunciation at Ohrid, and it is a masterpiece."

He reached out for the icon, but Zoë still held it tightly.

"Zoë, I've got my car here. We'll go straight to Belgrade. I want to examine it properly, show it to other scholars. We'll have it X-rayed, and get it cleaned by an expert. We'll display it in the National Museum under perfect lighting conditions. It will be one of our treasures, I promise you. Zoë, give me the icon."

"I wouldn't give it to them," cried Zoë. "And I won't give it to you!"

With a sudden twist, she broke loose from him and ran into the church with the icon still held aloft. Her halo of hair and the dark tones of her dress merged with the painted figures all around her, until it seemed as if she were one of them, broken loose from the confines of the walls. She ran straight to the central doors of the iconostasis, which women are forbidden to enter.

Petar, Stephen and Roger, all caught by surprise, hurried after her.

Just as she reached the iconostasis, the doors were flung open, and the abbot appeared. He said nothing at all, but at the sight of him, Petar, Stephen, and Roger stood still, none of them knowing why they should do so. Zoë, in one fluid, graceful movement, sank to her knees, and held up the icon toward him. He stretched out his hands in blessing over her head before he accepted it from her.

Then he stood in absolute silence, gazing steadily at the icon, while the girl knelt motionless with her head bowed.

"Does he know what it is?" Stephen said to Petar.

"I think he suspects the same as I do. Before the Turkish conquest, this monastery had a very great treasure. It was described in their Chronicle as a miracle-working icon of the Mother of God. Then, at the time of the conquest,

132

one runway, Geneva airport radioed the plane from Dubrovnik to divert it to another airport. Klaus and Heinrich had lost all sense of their whereabouts because of the heavy cloud cover. They knew nothing until they had actually landed and saw an airport sign saying "Basel." At least they were in the right country.

They were kept on the plane until everyone else had left, and the Yugoslav pilot came down to see them.

He said, "My instructions were to see you onto Swiss soil. Here you are. Here are your passports."

Heinrich was so nervous with sheer relief that he could hardly walk down the steps of the aircraft. They still had to pass through Swiss immigration on their false passports. The officials looked suspiciously at their unshaven appearance, but let them in.

They caught the first bus they could away from the airport, and mingled with the crowds in a cheap café in Basel. Then they took stock. All their luggage was in the car which was being shipped to Italy, and which they had signed for with false names and addresses. Their own passports were hidden in Milan, and they had lost most of their money. If anyone recognized them in their disguise it would be very hard indeed to explain what they were doing.

On the other hand, if they could resume their own identities quickly, they had the great advantage that no one would ever connect them with the scruffy pair who had just entered the country. Basel was not very far from their homes in Zürich. Klaus put through a call from a public telephone to one of the only two people in Switzerland who knew where he had gone. In carefully guarded terms he arranged that a car should come to collect them.

135

He then sat down to drink endless cups of black coffee, and, contrary to his usual careful habits, to chain-smoke. It would not have been true to say that he planned to live a blameless life from that moment, for he was too deeply involved with dishonesty and deception. What he did vow was that he would keep to matters he understood, which was planning operations and directing them from a distance. Furthermore, he would not branch out into other fields, but would stick to Italian pictures. His encounter with the Byzantine world had achieved nothing but disaster.

It took some time for the police at Geneva airport to realize that the plane had been diverted to Basel. When they telephoned Basel, they found that the plane had already landed, and the two men had been allowed to enter the country.

Before the Swiss police could be alerted to keep a lookout for them, it was necessary to get a better description. Someone suggested that the quickest way would be to approach Yugoslavia for this. The army in Titograd could have provided an excellent description within a few minutes, but since the approach had come from Starigrad police station, it was to Starigrad that the Swiss police applied.

Starigrad police station was in a jubilant mood, for Granddad had just arrived with the news that Zoë was safe. A motorcyclist was sent off in search of her, since she was the person who had seen the most of the men.

At the moment when he entered the empty farmhouse, a powerful but unmemorable Ford car drew up at a street corner in Basel, and Klaus and Heinrich climbed in. They were never caught.

136

There was a faint rush of air as Zoë fled from the church.

Oddly enough, it was Roger who hurried out to comfort her, and to tell her to rest in the shade. The others all stared at each other, and the abbot, as if the icon had suddenly become too heavy for him, placed it on a small desk like a lectern with a lantern suspended over it.

"Did Zoë know the story about the lost icon?" Petar asked the abbot accusingly.

"I certainly hadn't told her myself. And she would not have seen the Chronicle, because it is kept in a part of the monastery where women are not admitted."

"Was there a tradition about it?" asked Stephen. "Her grandfather knows all these old stories that were passed on by word of mouth."

"No, I made inquiries about that," said Petar. "It seems the tradition was lost. The only evidence was there in the manuscript, and, quite honestly, I would think that the abbot and one of the other monks and I myself are the only people in Starigrad at this moment who would be able to read it. You need a good knowledge of Old Slavonic and ancient handwriting. Zoë's a clever girl, I know, but she's studying economics."

"Then what put this idea about miracles into her head?" Stephen insisted.

"I can't imagine. Zoë doesn't believe in that sort of thing. She thinks it's all superstition. But something must have happened to her when she was missing to make her start talking like that. Have you any idea what it was?"

"I don't know," said Stephen uneasily. "All she will say is that she spent the night up in the mountains. Either

137

she honestly can't remember, or else she is determined to make herself forget."

"Then don't try to make her," the abbot said very sharply. "She is still in a state of shock and she needs to rest. And don't strain her further by making any demands yourselves. Leave her alone for the time being, Petar, and you, too, as well," he added to Stephen's surprise.

With a feeling that they had been dismissed, Stephen and Petar went out together into the sunlight, to the scent of herbs and flowers and the loud murmur of bees. Zoë was sitting on a low wall, stroking the monastery cat. She looked pale and drained, but somehow at peace with herself.

She paid no attention to them, so Petar began to ask Stephen about his plans for the rest of their stay in Yugoslavia. Stephen said that they hoped to go to the dam site near Ohrid, so Petar told him about the churches, monasteries, and old houses that he might visit there. It was, on both sides, a conversation aimed at the girl, to show her that they had other interests apart from her, but as such it failed to make any effect. Zoë sat there, stroking the cat, its fur warmed by the sunlight, as if the whole of her being was concentrated into the tips of her fingers. It was doubtful if she even knew they were there.

Roger, too, sat happily and thought about caves and climbing, and how the girls back at home would seem compared to the twins and Zoë.

Meanwhile the abbot, whose mind had been trained in complex thought, had already found three separate explanations as to why Zoë should have behaved so oddly. The fourth possibility was, of course, that the icon had really saved Zoë, in some way she would not reveal. That meant he had to face the idea that what he had claimed all his life to believe might in fact be literally true.

In the first totally humble gesture that he had ever made, he bent down and kissed the icon, in the place where the lips of other men, long since dead, had worn all the gold away.